The Big Bang

Paul Reynolds was in the school science laboratory, carefully measuring yellow powder into a beaker on a set of scales. He pushed his fair hair out of his eyes as he checked the formula he'd written on a piece of paper.

'What are you doing lurking here, Reynolds?' a voice boomed.

Paul whirled around, expecting to see a teacher. His best friend, Alex Katsonis, grinned at him from the doorway.

'Alex!' Paul hissed. 'If we get busted making gunpowder, we're in big trouble.'

'Chill out, man. I got it.' Alex opened the box of charcoal he had 'borrowed' from the art room. Paul took out a couple of sticks and crumbled them into a beaker on the scales. Alex peered at the piece of paper, puzzled. 'The formula says carbon. What's the charcoal for?'

'Charcoal *is* carbon, dumbo,' Paul said. 'No wonder you had to repeat this year. Don't you do any study?'

'Why should I? I've got you. I come up with the brilliant plans. You look after the details.'

In almost every way, the two Year 9 boys were opposites. Paul was tall, solidly built and neat. Alex was wiry with dark curly hair which, like his clothes, was always fashionably unkempt. Where Paul was quiet and thought before he acted, Alex was a motormouth who acted on impulse. In spite of their differences, they had become firm friends. Paul admired Alex's spirit and irreverence towards authority, and Alex respected Paul's brains.

Alex leaned casually back on the bench where a dark liquid bubbled in a flask over a Bunsen burner.

'Careful,' Paul warned. 'That's Katrina's distillation experiment.'

'Katrina's a nerd,' Alex sneered.

Katrina Muggleton was the brain of the science class and thought Alex was an idiot.

Paul mixed the charcoal and sulphur with some white powder and began grinding them in a mortar with a stone pestle. Alex peered over his shoulder. 'Are you sure this is going to work?'

'They've been making gunpowder this way for thousands of years,' Paul replied.

Alex rolled his eyes. 'Spare me the lecture. How big's the bang going to be?'

'Big enough to scare the pants off everyone at the camp.' Their science class was going on a weekend camp to observe a solar eclipse. They both grinned as they imagined the chaos their explosion would cause.

Paul finished grinding and poured the black powder into a plastic container on the bench. 'It's done. Let's get out of here. You put this stuff away. I'll clean up the bench.'

As Alex reached for the jars of chemicals, he bumped the distillation equipment. It toppled over. The flask hit the bench and shattered, spilling the liquid. The bunsen burner tipped over, igniting it. Paul turned to see flames racing towards the container of gunpowder. 'Alex! The gunpowder!'

Paul and Alex dived to the floor just as the flames engulfed the container. With a deafening bang, the gunpowder exploded.

Clouds of thick black smoke filled the room and a fire alarm went off. Paul scrambled to his feet, grabbed an extinguisher and started spraying the benchtop. Alex yanked a fire blanket from its container and beat at the flames. They had just got the fire out when Ms Gibson, their science teacher, raced in. Katrina was hot on her heels.

'It's OK, Miss,' Alex said quickly. 'We've got it out.'

Ms Gibson turned off the fire alarm. Katrina went to the bench and stared in dismay at her shattered equipment.

'What were you two doing in here?' Ms Gibson demanded.

Paul was about to speak when Alex started coughing loudly. 'Lucky break, Miss,' he wheezed. 'I wasn't feeling too good and Paul was helping me to the sick bay. We heard the explosion and all this smoke started pouring out, so we raced in and Paul grabbed the extinguisher.'

Ms Gibson looked angrily around the room. 'Did you see anyone in here?'

Alex started coughing again.

'We'd better get the nurse to take a look at you,' Ms Gibson decided. 'Can't have you missing the camp tomorrow. You both did well.'

She took Alex's arm and helped him towards the door. Alex looked back at Paul and winked. Paul saw Katrina staring at him and felt his face go red. 'Sorry about your experiment, Katrina.'

'I bought all my own chemicals,' she grumbled. 'They cost me twenty dollars.'

'I'd better go and get cleaned up,' Paul said guiltily and scurried out.

Katrina angrily started cleaning up. She noticed a charred piece of paper on the bench. The words 'GUNPOWDER FORMULA' were still visible.

Paul hurried downstairs laden with his overnight bag, daypack, sleeping bag and a cardboard box. He carefully deposited the load at the bottom of the stairs.

'Dad!' he yelled. 'I'm going to miss the bus. Christine, hurry up!'

Christine, Paul's nine-year-old sister, came out of her bedroom. 'I'm really glad you're going on the school camp,' she said, grinning. 'A whole weekend without you around.'

As Christine reached the bottom of the stairs, she stumbled over the cardboard box.

'Careful!' Paul snapped. 'That's my science project.'

'Then what did you put it there for, stupid?'

'That's enough, you two. Let's go.'

Paul and Christine looked up to see their father coming out of his study. He picked up the cardboard box and Paul's sleeping bag. As they headed for the door, the phone rang.

'Leave it, Dad,' Paul pleaded.

Brian put down the box and sleeping bag and picked up the receiver. 'Brian Reynolds ... Hi, Marie. What's up?'

Paul watched impatiently as his father listened.

—'Check them against the projections on my computer,' Brian suggested.

Paul pointed at his watch. 'Dad!'

Brian put his hand over the receiver. 'I'm in

charge of the research department, Paul. This is important.'

Paul stamped angrily out of the house.

Alex was on the footpath outside the school, looking anxiously up the street. The school bus behind him was filled with science students impatient to get going.

Ms Gibson stepped off the bus. 'Get on, Alex.'

'But Paul said he'd be here.'

'Sorry. We can't wait any longer.'

As they were about to board the bus, a car sped towards them and screeched to a halt. The car had a blue licence plate that read 'MAGNET'. Paul leaped out and rummaged through the car boot. 'Where's my sleeping bag?'

'Didn't I give it to you?' Brian asked Christine.

'Dad! You had it in your hand when the phone rang.'

Brian gave Paul an apologetic smile. 'Sorry.'

'Oh, no problem,' Paul said sarcastically, pulling his gear from the car. 'After I've frozen to death in the mountains, you can invent something to thaw me out and bring me back to life.'

'We'd better get going,' Ms Gibson said and headed for the bus.

'Remember, you're going on this camp to study, not to chase girls,' Brian joked.

Paul turned away in embarrassment and saw Alex pointing a video-camera at him. 'You didn't film that?'

Alex grinned and nodded. Paul made a grab for the camera but Alex danced away.

'Watch it! Pop will kill me if I break this.'

Alex raced onto the bus with Paul close behind. Brian and Christine waved as the bus pulled away but Paul ignored them.

As the bus headed towards the outskirts of the city, Alex pointed his video-camera out the window and filmed an industrial estate. The small screen on the back of the camera showed clouds of noxious-looking smoke billowing from rusting chimneys. Alex turned away from the depressing scene and pointed the camera at Paul, who was engrossed in a science fiction novel called *Time Vortex*.

'So tell us, Paul,' Alex said in a news reporter's voice, 'which girl are you interested in chasing?'

'Rack off,' Paul snarled.

'What about Katrina? She fancies you.'

The slim, studious-looking girl in the seat in front of them turned and glared at Alex. 'What would you know, dogbreath?' she snapped.

Alex was surprised by her anger. 'What's up with you today, Muggleton?'

'You and Paul owe me twenty bucks,' Katrina said in a low, menacing voice. 'I know what you were doing in the lab yesterday. You were making gunpowder.'

She held up the charred piece of paper.

'No way,' Alex protested. 'Paul and I would never do anything silly or irresponsible. You heard Ms Gibson. We saved the school. We're heroes.'

He looked at Paul, who had slid down in his seat, looking very guilty. 'Don't worry, mate,' he whispered. 'She can't prove a thing.'

Hoping that Alex was right, Paul pulled his Walkman out of his bumbag, put the headphones on and turned up the volume.

Two hours later, the bus pulled up at the school camp. It was built at the base of Mount Lara, in a thick eucalypt forest. Wooden buildings and huts made up three sides of a quadrangle. On the fourth side was a commando-style obstacle course, complete with a flying fox. As soon as Alex saw it, he ran over, grabbed the handles of the pulley and slid down the cable, crowing with delight.

'Alex! Get off there!' Ms Gibson yelled.

Alex dropped to the ground and joined the students gathered around the teacher. She pointed to buildings on opposite sides of the quadrangle. 'That's the boys' dormitory. And that's the girls'.'

Alex moaned with mock disappointment.

'Get yourselves settled. When you hear this, lunch will be served in the main building.' She pressed the trigger on a compressed-air horn and its wail echoed loudly through the still of the bush. 'After that we'll head up the mountain to inspect our observation point for tomorrow. Does anyone remember why we're here?'

Katrina put up her hand. 'To observe the

solar eclipse when the moon passes between the earth and the sun.'

'Good,' Ms Gibson said. 'Let's get moving. If we have time, I'll take you to visit a haunted cave.'

A ripple of excitement passed through the students.

'And bring your science projects with you,' Ms Gibson reminded them.

'What science project?' Alex asked anxiously.

'We had to build a camera obscura.' Paul's face fell. 'Oh no, Dad left that at home too.'

Alex looked puzzled. 'What's a camera obscura?'

'It's a pinhole camera, pinhead,' Katrina sneered. She headed for her dormitory, laughing.

After lunch, Ms Gibson led the way up a track through dense bush. Most of the students were loaded down with bags and pieces of equipment. Paul and Alex were empty-handed.

'The ancient Chinese believed that eclipses were caused by a dragon eating the sun,' Ms

Gibson told the class. 'They beat drums and gongs to scare the dragon away.'

They must have been idiots,' Alex scoffed.

'It always worked.'

The class laughed. Ms Gibson stopped in a clearing. 'OK, this is the place. Get out your science projects. No-one watches the eclipse tomorrow unless I've checked their viewing equipment.'

Alex watched the other students getting to work. 'What are we going to do?' he asked Paul.

'A camera obscura is easy enough to make. We just need cardboard, plastic and tape.'

Alex looked at Katrina and her friend, Lisa, who were unpacking a large amount of equipment. 'They brought a lot of stuff.'

'There's no point in asking them.'

'Who said anything about asking?' Alex suddenly started yelling. 'Snake! A snake!'

The students dropped what they were doing and looked around. Ms Gibson hurried over to Alex. 'Where?'

'There. It was huge.'

Alex pointed towards some trees. Ms Gibson

moved cautiously forward. While everyone was watching her, Alex grabbed two shoe boxes, a plastic milk bottle and a roll of tape from Katrina's supply. He scurried behind some rocks as Ms Gibson came back.

'It's gone now,' she announced. 'But keep a lookout, all of you.'

Paul followed Alex behind the rocks.

'Come on, Einstein,' Alex said, holding up his booty. 'Show me what to do.'

By mid-afternoon, the clearing was filled with a variety of eclipse viewing equipment. Everyone was gathered around a tepee that Katrina and Lisa had erected. Inside, a telescope was hanging over a piece of white card, balanced against a box.

'The lens will project the image of the eclipse onto the viewing surface,' Katrina explained.

The card fell off the box. Annoyed, Katrina replaced it. 'Sorry, miss. We couldn't finish it properly because someone stole our tape.'

'Never mind. You've done very well.' Ms

Gibson put a tick against their names in her book. 'That's everybody except Paul and Alex. Where are those two?'

'I don't think they did a project,' Lisa said, smirking.

Ms Gibson looked around. 'Paul? Alex?'

'Over here!' Paul stepped out from behind the rocks. The students followed Ms Gibson over to him.

'Ladies and gentlemen,' Paul began in a spruiker's voice. 'The House of Paul and Alex takes great pleasure in presenting ... the Camera Obscura Cap.'

Alex strutted from behind the rocks like a fashion model. One of the stolen shoe boxes was taped under the peak of his baseball cap so that it hung in front of his face like a huge nose. He looked ridiculous and the students laughed.

Paul put on an identical cap and tilted his head to look at the sun. A small hole in the end of the shoe box projected an image of the sun onto a piece of milk bottle plastic in front of his eyes.

'Note how the stylish Camera Cap allows the wearer to safely observe the eclipse while leaving the hands free to write notes and draw diagrams,' Paul explained.

'And pick their nose,' Alex said, sticking a finger up his nostril. There was more laughter.

'It's safe,' Paul finished, 'cheap and environmentally friendly.'

'And extremely spunky,' Alex added, striking a sexy pose.

The class applauded. Alex and Paul looked very pleased with themselves as Ms Gibson ticked their names. Katrina didn't look pleased at all. Especially when she saw her roll of tape on the ground nearby.

The students were subdued as Ms Gibson led them towards the haunted cave. The bush was eerily quiet except for the faint electrical hum of the high-tension power lines that ran overhead.

'The early explorers reported seeing strange lights around this cave,' Ms Gibson said quietly. 'Ever since, there have been stories of the mysterious Mount Lara lights.'

'Miss, is the cave really haunted?' Lisa asked nervously.

'The locals thought so. But when these power lines were put up, engineers discovered magnetic rocks all through the mountain.'

Ms Gibson held up a compass. The needle spun wildly. 'See? The cave is the focus of a powerful magnetic field.'

'So the lights are just an electro-magnetic effect?' Paul asked.

'Probably. But no-one's ever been able to get a photograph of them.'

Ms Gibson took out a torch and called into the cave. 'If there are any ghosts in there, you'd better watch out. Year 9 is coming in. You don't stand a chance.'

The students followed her into the cave. The inside was a disappointment. There was nothing weird at all.

'Maybe the ghosts only come out at night,' Ms Gibson joked.

Her torch beam illuminated a patch of white crystals encrusting the roof of the cave. 'Does anyone know what this is?' she asked.

'Bat poo?' Alex suggested.

'Let's see.' Ms Gibson licked a finger, ran it across the crystals and then put it in her mouth. The class groaned with disgust.

Ms Gibson smiled. 'No, bat poo tastes better. This is potassium nitrate. Otherwise known as ...?'

Katrina stuck up her hand. 'Saltpetre, miss.'

'It's used to make gunpowder,' Alex said, hoping to score some points off Katrina.

'Good,' said Ms Gibson, surprised by Alex's knowledge. 'Can anyone tell me the other chemical components of gunpowder?'

Paul elbowed Alex before he could say more. Katrina nudged him and held up the charred piece of paper with the gunpowder formula on it. Alex ignored her.

'Paul can, miss,' Katrina said loudly.

Ms Gibson looked at Paul who looked desperately at Alex. Alex handed Katrina a twenty-dollar note and she gave him the piece of paper. Alex swallowed it.

'I know, miss,' Katrina said. 'The other components are sulphur and charcoal.'

'Well done, Katrina.'

Alex scowled as Katrina smiled victoriously.

'You can't take my camera,' Lisa protested as

she and Katrina walked back to their hut after dinner.

'Then you'll have to come to the cave with me.'

'At midnight? No way!'

'Lisa,' Katrina said firmly, 'there's nothing to be scared of. And if we can photograph the Lara lights, we'll be famous.'

'But what if they're caused by ghosts?'

'There's no such thing as ghosts!'

As they went into their hut, Alex and Paul emerged from the shadows.

'Let's make sure there really is a ghost,' Alex suggested with a devilish grin. 'They'll freak out and I'll catch it all on video.'

Paul didn't look keen.

'Katrina deserves it,' Alex said. 'Nobody blackmails a Katsonis and gets away with it.'

'You're even now. Why don't you leave her alone?'

Alex looked suspiciously at Paul. 'You've got the hots for her, haven't you?'

'You're out of your skull,' Paul exclaimed.

Alex smirked. 'Paul and Katrina. Wait till that gets around.'

Paul knew Alex wouldn't let up until he agreed. 'All right. I'll come.'

At ten minutes to midnight, Alex sat perched in a fork of a tree near the cave. He was tying a white sheet to the flying fox pulley that he and Paul had taken from the camp, along with the steel cable. The cable was secured around a tree branch and ran down to the cave mouth, where it was anchored to a rock.

Paul stood at the base of the tree, shining a torch up into the branches. The video-camera, a second torch and Ms Gibson's air-horn lay beside his backpack on the ground. Paul was wearing a dark shirt over a black T-shirt printed with a grinning skull. Both boys' faces were blackened with burnt cork.

'Bring up the other torch,' Alex called.

Paul stuck the torch in the belt of his bumbag and leaped up to the lowest branch. His runners slipped on the trunk and Paul fell heavily to the ground. He yelped.

'Are you OK?' Alex called.

'I've cut my hand.'

'Are you bleeding to death?'

'No.'

'Then hurry up!'

Paul wrapped a handkerchief around his hand, and awkwardly shinned up the tree.

Alex held the sheet while Paul tied the torch to the pulley inside it. He turned it on and two holes cut in the sheet glowed like eyes. Paul and Alex smiled at their ghost.

Paul became aware of the electrical hum in the air and looked up nervously. 'We should move the cable. It's too close to the power lines.'

'It'll be fine.' Alex said.

He saw a light flickering down the trail. 'They're coming. I'll hide in the cave. Wait for my signal.'

Alex quickly scrambled down the tree. Paul unwrapped the bloodied handkerchief and examined his cut by the torchlight.

'Turn off the torch, dummy!' Alex called. He picked up the video-camera and air-horn and ran to the cave.

Paul switched off the torch and lost his balance in the sudden darkness. He grabbed the branch to steady himself and dropped his handkerchief, which blew away into the night.

Katrina and Lisa appeared at the top of the trail.

'I don't like this place,' Lisa whispered nervously.

'How many times do I have to tell you?' Katrina said impatiently. 'There's no such thing as ghosts.'

Inside the cave, Alex started the video-camera rolling as Katrina and Lisa approached.

'What was going on between you and Paul this afternoon?' Lisa asked, trying to take her mind off her fear.

'Nothing.'

Lisa nudged her friend. 'Come on, Kat. You can tell me. You like him, don't you?'

Katrina smiled. 'Well, he is kind of cute.'

Alex couldn't believe his luck. He was getting all this on tape. He stepped back, knocking over the air-horn. The metal can clattered on the rocks.

'Who's there?' Katrina called.

In the tree, Paul realised that Alex was about to be discovered. He moaned loudly.

Lisa whirled round. 'What was that?'

'I don't know.' Katrina tried to sound unconcerned. 'It was probably just an animal.'

Paul let out another moan.

'That was no animal,' Lisa said, on the verge of panic. 'Can we go back?'

'No. I want to see the lights.'

In the cave, Alex flicked the torch on and off. Lisa saw the glow. Too terrified to speak, she grabbed Katrina and pointed. Katrina excitedly lifted her camera.

Alex pressed the trigger on the air-horn and a loud screech blasted from the cave. Katrina and Lisa stumbled backwards in fear.

In the tree, Paul turned on the torch inside the sheet, but as he launched the ghost down the cable, he lost his footing. As he fell, he grabbed the torch and found himself hurtling down the cable, hanging beneath the sheet. He screeched in fear.

The girls whirled around and saw a ghost flying towards them, eyes blazing, wailing like a banshee. Lisa screamed and fled back down the trail.

As Paul swooped towards the cave, the torch broke away from the pulley and Paul crashed to the ground near Katrina.

She raced over and lifted the sheet. 'Paul?' she said in surprise.

Alex came out of the cave, laughing hysterically. Katrina saw him and realised what was going on. 'That was so dumb,' she said angrily. 'You never fooled me for a second.'

'We did,' Alex smirked, holding up the video-camera. 'It's all captured on film. And guess what, Paul? Katrina thinks you're cute.'

'Give me that!' Katrina yelled.

'It'll cost you forty bucks,' Alex gloated.

Paul grabbed the camera and put it in his pack. 'We'd better get back before Lisa wakes up the camp.'

As Paul shouldered his pack, electricity began crackling around the high-tension wires above them. Sparks of energy flashed around the cave mouth, creating a rippling curtain of energy. There was a tearing sound and a rip appeared in the air.

Katrina stared at the weird sight in astonishment. 'How are you guys doing that?'

'We're not,' Paul answered.

The rip became wider. Through it could be

seen a rusted metal stand, topped by what looked like a satellite dish. Electricity crackled between the dish and a huge metal tower behind it.

Paul edged closer. He reached out and put his hand through the rip in the curtain of energy.

'Be careful!' Katrina warned.

There was a loud snap of electricity that made Alex's hair stand on end. He looked up and saw a massive bolt of energy jump from the power lines to the flying fox cable. 'Paul, look out,' he yelled and dived to the ground. Katrina did the same.

The bolt of energy surged down the cable and surrounded Paul. Katrina lifted her head. There was a blinding flash of light. When her vision cleared, Paul was gone.

Paul staggered away from the rip in the energy curtain and stumbled into the metal dish. Something dropped out of it and the curtain started to fade.

Dazed and shaken, Paul looked around. Electricity crackled around the top of a tall tower of rusting metal. Paul rubbed his eyes. What was going on?

'Alex? Katrina?' he called.

There was no reply. Paul looked down and saw a slim octagonal box on the ground. He picked it up. It was metallic and the top was carved with a design of two intertwined snakes over the face of a sun. As Paul attempted to open it, a tall man stepped out of the darkness. He was wearing a rough woven tunic and a strange black hat which was wider at the top than the bottom.

'Drop that,' the man ordered.

Paul whirled around and the man gasped in fear. 'Marauder!' he cried, pointing to the skull on Paul's T-shirt. 'Return my Eyestone!'

The man made a grab for Paul. Frightened and bewildered, Paul dodged away but the man grabbed his pack. Paul struggled and his arms came out of the straps. He ran for his life.

'Alex! Where are you?' Paul yelled as he stumbled through the darkness. 'There's a lunatic up here!'

The man suddenly raced from behind a rock, swinging a tree branch like a club. Paul fled blindly downhill, crashing through bushes and over logs in his desperate flight. He tripped over a rock and lay still, listening. The sounds of pursuit faded. Paul crawled to the base of a tree and huddled against it. His mind was racing. What was happening to him? Where were Alex and Katrina? He looked down and saw he was still clutching the metal object which the madman had called an Eyestone.

'Paul! ... Paul!'

Alex's voice echoed around the hillside. He came out of the bush and looked anxiously at Katrina. 'I can't find him.'

'I told you,' Katrina said. 'He just disappeared.'

'That's impossible.'

'Then where is he?'

'He must have got electrocuted.'

'Where's the body? There'd at least be some ash.'

'Katrina!'

They looked at each other in silence.

'We have to tell Ms Gibson,' Katrina said at last.

Alex went pale. 'What are we going to say?'

Morning sunlight filtered through a thick canopy of trees onto a mound of leaves. From inside the mound came the beep of a digital watch alarm. There was movement under the leaves, then Paul sat up. He looked around, wondering where he was. He saw the Eyestone on the ground and realised in dismay that he hadn't been dreaming.

Paul picked up the Eyestone and scrambled to his feet, looking round nervously. 'Alex! Katrina! Anyone!' he yelled, his voice echoing around the hills.

There was no answer. Paul unzipped his bumbag and took out his Walkman. He put on the headphones and tried to tune into a radio station. The airwaves were silent.

Paul was starting to feel that something was

seriously wrong. He looked down the thickly wooded slope. A thin column of smoke was rising into the air. Hoping that the smoke came from the school camp, he raced down the slope towards it.

Paul scrambled out of the undergrowth and emerged onto the bank of a wide river. A small campfire was burning in a clearing. Next to the fire were what looked like bundles of clothes and animal skins. 'Hello! Is anyone here?' Paul called.

He heard a whirring sound and looked around. A set of weighted cords flew through the air and wrapped around his torso, pinning his arms to his sides. Paul realised with a shock that he'd been hit by bolas. They were attached to a long cord which ran into the trees. As Paul struggled to get free, the cord was yanked, pulling him off his feet.

A lithe figure wearing a hooded cloak ran from the trees, grabbed a burning branch from the fire and stood over Paul, pointing it at his face. Paul felt the heat searing his cheek. He stopped struggling and stared up in fear.

Where Am I?

'Please don't hurt me,' Paul pleaded as he tried to squirm away from the burning branch.

The figure standing over him threw back its cloak and Paul found himself staring into the determined face of a pretty teenage girl. She had startling green eyes and her blond hair was tied back in a ponytail. With her rough green tunic and leggings, Paul thought she looked like a character from a Robin Hood movie.

'You're just a girl,' Paul said, relieved.

He tried to sit up but the girl pushed him down with her foot.

'Lie still, Marauder,' she said in a strange accent.

'I'm not a marauder,' Paul protested. 'I don't even know what a marauder is.'

The girl dragged Paul to his feet and picked

up her bundles. 'Start walking,' she ordered, yanking on the rope.

Still bound by the bolas, Paul stumbled along the narrow track beside the fast-flowing river. 'Where are we going?' he asked.

The girl said nothing.

'Look, if I've trespassed on your land, I'm sorry. I got lost last night. I'm from the school camp. If you take me there, they'll tell you who I am.'

The girl kept walking, forcing Paul to follow.

'My father is an important scientist,' Paul said, trying another tack. 'If you bring me back, I'll make sure he gives you a reward.'

The girl still wouldn't respond.

'Listen, you stupid girl,' Paul yelled, losing his patience. 'Kidnapping's illegal. If you don't let me go right now, you're in big trouble.'

Suddenly the birds stopped singing. The forest became eerily silent as the sky darkened. The girl looked up and saw a black circle moving across the face of the sun. 'The Darkness,' she whispered in horror. 'You've brought the Darkness!'

The gloom deepened. The girl stared at Paul,

her face a mask of terror. 'Please, Marauder, bring back the sun.'

'It's an eclipse,' Paul explained, wondering why the girl was so scared. 'Don't you go to school? It's just the moon passing in front of the sun.'

The girl looked up.

'Don't stare at it,' Paul shouted.

She quickly looked away.

'Please don't destroy the world,' she pleaded. 'I'm sorry for hurting you. Bring back the sun. Please, bring it back.'

Paul saw his opportunity. 'I will if you untie me.'

The girl did as he asked. She coiled up the bolas and hung them from her belt. 'When will you bring back the sun?'

'Any second now.' Paul pointed upwards. 'Let there be light!'

The girl looked up and saw the edge of the sun reappear. Birds began twittering again.

'Thank you, Marauder,' the girl said, relief and gratitude suffusing her face.

'I'm not a marauder. Look, here's what happened.' Paul squatted and started to draw a diagram in the dirt with his finger. 'An eclipse is when the moon's orbit brings it in conjunction with the sun.'

He looked up to see if the girl was listening. She wasn't. She was running along the trail towards a narrow rope bridge crossing the river. As she leaped onto the bridge and began to cross, the structure swayed alarmingly. Paul ran towards her. 'Wait. You have to take me to the school camp!'

The girl kept moving. Paul started to cross, moving awkwardly as he tried to keep his balance on the thin wooden slats of the swinging bridge. He fell against the side ropes and the whole bridge twisted. The sudden movement threw the girl into the water.

Paul hung between the swaying ropes, looking down at the girl floundering in the deep water. He realised that she was being pulled down by the bundles on her back. 'Hang on,' he called. 'I'm coming!'

Paul tried a dive but the bridge swayed and he tumbled into the river. He surfaced, gasping from the shock of the cold water. The girl was close by, desperately trying to stay afloat. Paul grabbed her arm but she pushed him away.

'I'm trying to save you,' Paul yelled, grabbing the bundles. 'Help me. Kick your legs.'

Paul swam with all his strength. The girl started to kick and they slowly made their way to safety.

The girl collapsed on the grassy bank, coughing up water. Paul sat down nearby, panting. He groaned as he noticed that the face of his digital watch was blank. Water had got inside.

'Why did you save my life, Marauder?' the girl asked.

'What is this "marauder" thing? What are you talking about?'

The girl looked at him warily.

'Look,' he said gently, 'I'm Paul. What's your name?'

She didn't answer.

'I just saved your life. At least you could tell me your name.'

The girl shook her head.

'OK, just tell me the way to the city.'

The girl looked puzzled. 'City?'

'Yeah, the city. Sydney. Heap big town on

other side of mountains.'

The girl stared at Paul. 'Have you escaped from the Spellbinders?'

Now it was Paul's turn to be puzzled. 'What are Spellbinders?'

The girl gave him a disbelieving look.

'I had an accident last night,' Paul explained. 'My friends will be looking for me. Can you take me to a telephone?'

'Telephone?' she echoed.

'You know, a telephone.' He mimed the action of making a call. 'You pick up the receiver, you dial the number, then you talk to people a long way away.'

The girl grabbed her sodden bundles and got quickly to her feet. 'You're mad. Only the Spellbinders can do that.'

'Who are these stupid Spellbinders?' Paul snapped.

The girl backed away. Paul grabbed one of the bundles. 'Just take me to the highway,' he pleaded. 'I'll flag down a car.'

The girl let go of the bundle and ran towards the bridge. 'Don't go,' Paul yelled. 'I'm lost.'

The girl was halfway across the bridge by

the time Paul reached it.

'Wait,' he cried. 'Don't you want these?' He held up the bundle but the girl ran into the trees on the other side of the river. He dropped the bundle and it came apart. Paul saw that the skins and cloth had been fashioned into cloaks. Quickly retying the bundle, he went after the girl, but by the time he reached the other side of the bridge, she was gone.

The mid-morning sun beat down as Paul trudged up a steep wooded slope. Where was the school camp? All he could see was trees and they didn't look like the ones he remembered around Mount Lara.

He heard voices and hurried up the slope. Two sweating men were pulling sleds along a track. The sleds were laden with large red sacks, each one marked with the same intertwined snake symbol which Paul had seen carved on the Eyestone.

Paul was about to step out of the trees when two hideous-looking creatures rose up from the forest floor. Vegetation seemed to grow from their misshapen bodies. Paul wondered if they were mutants.

The creatures lumbered onto the track, each one whirling a heavy wooden blade on the end of a rope. They produced a menacing sound. Paul recognised them as bullroarers.

The men looked round in terror.

'Marauders! Bron, come on!' one yelled. He dropped his sled and fled into the forest.

The other man stood his ground. Another Marauder dropped out of a tree with a net, knocking the man to the ground.

The Marauders dragged the loaded sleds into the trees. They blended so well into the undergrowth that in a moment they had vanished completely.

His head spinning, Paul hurried to the man lying under the net. His leg was twisted beneath him. 'Are you all right?' Paul asked.

The man groaned.

'Get away from him, Marauder!'

Paul turned and saw the other man coming out of the trees, brandishing a thick branch. The man charged, yelling. Paul ran for his life.

The bush echoed with shouts as students from the science camp helped the police rescue squad in the search for Paul.

Brian Reynolds, Paul's worried father, had just arrived from the city, accompanied by two policemen.

'Then the electricity came down the cable,' Alex explained, pointing up at the cable that still ran from the tree to the cave. 'I jumped out of the way. That was the last I saw of him.'

'What the hell were you doing hanging a steel cable near power lines?' Brian asked angrily.

'I'm sorry, Mr Reynolds. It was just a prank to scare the girls. No-one was supposed to get hurt.'

'It's a bit late for that,' Brian snapped. 'Paul could be lying at the bottom of a cliff with a broken neck!'

There was an awkward silence. Alex looked uncomfortably at Katrina and Lisa, wondering if he had caused the death of his best friend.

'Maybe the ghost took him,' Lisa suggested.

The sergeant stared at her. 'What ghost?'

'Last night, Katrina and I saw a ghost in the cave.'

The constable turned on his torch and went into the cave.

'There was no ghost,' Katrina said. 'Paul and Alex were just trying to scare us. Then there was this huge flash of light and Paul just disappeared.'

'Katrina, Paul can't have just vanished,' Ms Gibson said.

'It's true. Tell them, Alex!'

Everyone looked at Alex. 'I didn't see it,' he said awkwardly.

Katrina stared at him. 'Alex!'

'I didn't!'

There was a ghostly moan from the cave and everyone turned. The constable emerged holding the white sheet. 'I think I've found our ghost,' he said, shining his torch though the eyeholes.

The sergeant looked suspiciously at Alex and Katrina. 'Are you kids trying to pull some kind of hoax?'

Paul peered in amazement through some bushes at a crowd of people walking along a dirt road. They were all dressed like the girl from the river, in homespun tunics and dresses, and all spoke with the same strange accent. Some carried bundles of skins and other wares. Others dragged sleds laden with fruit and vegetables.

The road led to a bend in a wide river. Rafts and barges were moored at the bank which was covered with brightly coloured tents and stalls. Paul wondered if he had come upon some kind of hippy festival.

The crowd parted and Paul saw the tall man with the strange black hat who had chased him the night before. He was hurrying towards the market, carrying Paul's pack. A burly sentry was inspecting everyone going into the market. The sentry bowed respectfully and let the man pass.

Paul remembered that Alex's expensive video-camera was in the pack. Not wanting to look out of place, Paul pulled a cloak from the girl's bundle and put it on. Looking like one of the crowd, Paul stepped onto the road and joined the line headed into the market.

The sentry gave Paul a cursory glance and waved him past. Keeping the cloak wrapped tightly around him, Paul walked into the market. He caught sight of the tall man between some stalls and hurried after him. The man made his way towards an ornate red tent, its sides emblazoned with the snake symbol. A young man in a uniform also bearing the snake symbol sat at a table outside the tent making marks in a book as people piled sacks of grain and other goods before him.

Then a whisper raced through the crowd and the market suddenly became quiet. Paul saw a woman with flaming red hair riding a black horse. She was wearing a heavy black jacket studded with gleaming copper fittings. As she approached everyone dropped to their knees. Paul remained standing.

A youth grabbed Paul's arm and pulled him down. 'Are you crazy or just stupid?' the youth asked.

The woman rode up to the tent and dismounted. The uniformed youth and the man with Paul's pack bowed. No-one in the crowd moved. Then three laughing children ran around the side of the tent. One girl collided with the woman and the crowd gasped. Fear flashed in the girl's eyes and she quickly dropped to her knees.

'Whose child is this?' the woman called.

The girl's mother got quickly to her feet.

The red-headed woman picked up the girl. 'Were you frightened by the Darkness this morning, little one?'

The child nodded.

'Today, the Marauders tried again to bring an end to our world,' the woman told the crowd in a powerful voice. 'But we Spellbinders cast a mighty spell and brought back the sun.'

So this was a Spellbinder, Paul thought. He couldn't understand why no-one laughed at her. Surely they didn't believe in magic?

'Praise the Spellbinders!' called the young uniformed man.

'Praise the Spellbinders!' the crowd repeated.

The woman handed the girl back to her mother and strode into her tent. The two men followed her. People started getting to their feet.

Paul sneaked down the side of the red tent. Pretending to be admiring the view of the river, he stepped back against the canvas. Inside, he could hear voices.

'It was hideous!' the older man was saying. 'It appeared in a flash of light and stole my Eyestone.'

'And this Marauder had two heads, Summoner?' the woman interrupted.

'Yes, Spellbinder. One on its shoulders and a skull growing from its chest.' With a smile, Paul realised the man was referring to the skull printed on his T-shirt.

Suddenly Paul was grabbed from behind.

'Do you want to be banished to the Wastelands, boy?' the sentry bellowed. Paul shook his head. 'Then don't let me see you here again.'

The sentry applied a large boot to Paul's backside and Paul staggered into the marketplace. He passed a stall displaying bone knives with carved wooden handles. He looked around and realised that everything in the market was made of cloth or bone or wood. There was nothing made of metal and absolutely no sign of twentieth-century technology. Where was he? More importantly, *when* was he?

Paul heard a familiar voice and looked across the market. The girl who had captured him was standing behind a stall, trying to sell a cloak to a woman with a child.

'Don't you have anything smaller?' the woman asked, holding a large cloak around her daughter's narrow shoulders.

'No,' the girl said. 'I lost them on the way here. But I can make you one for the next market.'

The woman shook her head and put the cloak down.

'Try one of these.'

The girl stared in surprise as Paul spread his bundle of cloaks on the stall. 'Go away!' she hissed.

She turned her back on Paul and smiled at the woman, who was trying one of the cloaks on her daughter. 'That one looks nice.'

'It smells damp,' the woman said. 'I'll swap you a smoked fish for it.'

'It'll dry out,' Paul said enthusiastically. 'And there's a lot of workmanship in that cloak. It'll last her for years.'

'What about the basket?' the woman asked.

'It's a good swap,' the girl said quickly.

The woman handed over a large woven basket and walked off with her daughter and the new cloak. The girl turned to Paul, who was smiling at his success.

'Go away.'

'What year is this?' Paul asked.

'Why do you keep asking questions?' the girl said testily.

'Because I think I've worked out what's happened to me. I've gone back in time. I must have fallen through a time vortex or something. This must be medieval England.'

'Quiet!' the girl hissed, a look of alarm on her face. 'You look strange and you talk nonsense. I don't want the Spellbinder to think I know you. Now go away!'

'Please,' he said. 'You're the only person I know here. I'm lost. I'm hungry.'

'Then barter something for some food.'

'I don't have anything.' Paul held out his

empty hands.

The girl pushed up his sleeve and pointed to the broken digital watch on his wrist.

Plump sausages sizzled over an open fire. Paul watched, his mouth watering, as a red-faced cook admired the watch which was now strapped on his wrist. 'My wife likes trinkets,' he said. 'It's a good swap.'

He handed Paul a large sausage sandwiched between thick slices of bread. Paul sniffed it hungrily. 'It's a very good swap,' Paul agreed, taking a huge bite.

As Paul walked through the market eating, he was hit in the chest by a flying toy. He picked it up.

The youth who had earlier pulled him to the ground hurried over. 'I'm sorry. It doesn't work very well yet.'

Paul examined the toy. Its body and wings were bird-shaped and a fin protruded from its belly. It had a carved wooden propeller which was powered by twisted gut. 'Did you make this?' he asked the youth.

'Yes. But I can't make it fly straight.'

'It needs a rudder.'

'What's a rudder?'

'Like a bird's tail. To keep it stable. You could use this.' Paul pointed to the fin. 'Can I show you?'

The youth nodded, watching intently as Paul began to remove the fin.

'I'm Paul.'

'My name is Zander,' the youth replied. 'Where are you from?'

'A very long way away.'

Paul carefully pushed the fin into the tail of the toy. 'It would have more lift if I could put flaps on the wings, but this should help it fly straighter.'

Zander looked at him curiously. 'Where did you learn about flying?'

'From my father. He's a scientist.'

'A what?'

'A scientist. He invents new things.'

Zander looked at Paul in alarm. 'Is he a Spellbinder?'

Paul laughed. 'We don't have Spellbinders where I come from.'

'Where is that?'

'In the future.'

Zander stared at Paul as though he was mad.

Paul handed over the finished toy. 'Come on, let's see if this baby flies.'

Zander wound the propeller and launched the toy. It soared into the air, flying straight and true. Children stared at it in amazement. Zander smiled at Paul in delight.

Suddenly a ball of energy sizzled through the air and hit the flying toy. It burst into flames and fell to the ground. Paul and Zander turned to see the Spellbinder standing outside her tent. Sparks of energy were crackling around the tips of her fingers.

Everyone in the market dropped to their knees. Zander again pulled Paul to the ground. The young man in the uniform picked up the smouldering toy and took it to the Spellbinder. She addressed the silent crowd in an imperious voice. 'Who made this?'

Heads turned to Paul and Zander.

'Stay down!' Zander whispered. Then he leaped to his feet and started to run.

The Spellbinder struck her wrists together and a spark of energy flashed between them.

She pointed her right arm at Zander and a ball of energy flashed from her fingers. It flew across the marketplace and hit Zander as he ran. Power crackled around his body: he collapsed to the ground.

Paul stared at the Spellbinder, his mind reeling. There were no laser beams in the past. Was the woman a witch?

Two sentries dragged Zander to the Spellbinder.

'It is forbidden to build new things,' she told the crowd. 'This boy has broken Spellbinder law. He must be punished. Apprentice, take him to my tent.'

The young man in uniform beckoned to the sentries, who dragged Zander into the tent. The Spellbinder was about to follow when the red-faced cook pointed at Paul. 'Spellbinder, that boy was helping him.'

The Spellbinder fixed Paul with a steely gaze. 'Stand, boy.'

Paul got to his feet. 'Look, I'm sorry. I didn't know your laws. I'm new here.'

'Bring him!' the Spellbinder commanded.

The cook grabbed Paul's cloak. Paul twisted

out of it and the cook stared at the skull on his T-shirt. 'Marauder,' he yelled and leaped away.

A woman screamed. Before Paul could escape, a bolt of energy shot from the Spellbinder's fingers and hit him. Energy crackled over Paul's body but to his surprise, he felt nothing. The Spellbinder gaped as Paul fled across the marketplace. 'Seize the Marauder,' she commanded.

The cook and some other men started chasing Paul. He dived under a stall covered in vegetables. He upended it in his pursuers' path and scrambled between two tents.

Paul raced past the backs of stalls, leaping over baskets of produce as he tried to escape. He found himself at the rear of the Spell-binder's tent. The sounds of pursuit were getting louder. Paul dropped to the ground and rolled under the canvas.

He looked around the inside of the tent. He was lying behind a large couch. He peered around it and saw Zander cowering on his knees. The Spellbinder's Apprentice and the Summoner, the man in the black hat, stood over him. Paul's pack was on a nearby table.

The tent flap was pushed aside and the Spellbinder strode in. The Apprentice and the Summoner quickly bowed. While their heads were lowered, Paul grabbed his pack and rolled beneath the couch.

'The two-headed Marauder is in the market,' the Spellbinder said. 'My power suit couldn't stop it. Gryvon, show me the Marauder's possessions.'

The Apprentice stared at the empty table. 'I put its bag down there. Where's it gone?'

The Summoner looked around nervously. 'The Marauder must have stolen it back!'

The Spellbinder went over to Zander. 'What do you know of this Marauder?'

'Nothing, Spellbinder.'

While no-one was looking, Paul slid out from under the couch and rolled back under the tent wall, pulling his pack after him.

Brian Reynolds stood on the hillside above the cave, scanning the bush with a pair of binoculars. Alex and Katrina were sitting outside the cave, looking tired and worried. They looked up as a policeman hurried out of the bush shouting, 'Mr Reynolds! Mr Reynolds!'

Alex and Katrina leaped to their feet and Brian scrambled down the hillside.

'Mr Reynolds, do you recognise this?' The constable held out a bloodstained hand-kerchief.

Brian took it and stared at the P embroidered in the corner. 'It's Paul's. My God, he's injured!'

'Take it easy, Mr Reynolds,' Alex said. 'Paul scratched himself while he was climbing the tree last night.'

'Where did you find it?' Brian asked the constable.

'Down the mountain. Your son is probably in shock and dropped it as he wandered away. It's a good sign. I'm sure we'll find him soon.'

'See? Everything's going to be alright,' Alex told Katrina. 'You must have imagined it.'

Katrina nodded her head. But in her heart, she wasn't so sure.

Night had settled over the marketplace which was lit by flaming torches and fires. Paul lay at the bottom of a barge on the river under a pile of grain sacks. He had been there for hours as a search party combed the riverbank.

Paul buried himself deeper under the sacks when two youths climbed onto the barge. When one of them started poking around the sacks with a sharp boat-hook, Paul realised it was only a matter of time before he was discovered. He carefully opened his pack, took out the torch and shone the beam on the side of the boat.

'What's that?' asked one of the boys.

The other shrugged. 'Touch it.'

'No, you touch it.'

As they moved towards the light, Paul shifted the torch and the circle slid along the side of the boat. The boys jumped back in fright.

'It's a Marauder light,' yelled the first one. 'Let's catch it! We might get a reward.' He picked up a bucket and tried to sneak up on the light. Paul moved the torch beam onto the boy's body.

'It's on me!' the boy screamed. 'Get it off! Get it off!'

As his mate went to help, Paul moved the beam again. 'It's on me!' screeched the second boy. 'Help!'

Paul grinned as the frightened youths fled across the boats towards the bank. Suddenly a meaty hand hauled him to his feet and Paul found himself staring into the menacing face of the cook.

Paul shone the torch in the cook's eyes. Blinded, he let Paul go. Paul pulled the air-horn from his pack and fired a blast. The cook clapped his hands over his ears and staggered backwards. He tripped over the side of the barge and plunged into the river. The splash made the boys look back. 'There it is!' one yelled, pointing to Paul.

Paul ran across a gangplank to the shore. As he raced between two tents, a figure tackled him to the ground. Paul struggled hard, until he realised it was the girl with the cloaks. She pushed Paul into the shadows of a tent just as the two youths appeared.

'The Marauder knocked me down,' the girl

panted to them. 'It went that way.' She pointed across the market and the boys ran off. Paul emerged from the shadows and the girl held out a cloak. 'Put this on and follow me.' She picked up her basket and bundles from beside the tent and ran towards the trees. Paul followed.

In spite of the darkness, the girl moved easily through the thick forest. Paul stumbled over roots and banged into branches as he tried to keep up with her.

'Why did you decide to help me?' he asked.

'You saved my life and returned my cloaks,' the girl replied. 'A Marauder would not have done those things.'

'I'd thank you,' Paul said, 'but I still don't know your name.'

'Riana.'

'Thank you, Riana.'

Riana looked at him curiously. 'Why didn't the Spellbinder's power hurt you?'

'I don't know,' Paul replied. That had been puzzling him too.

They reached the top of a rise. Below, the calm surface of the river sparkled in the moonlight. 'Once across the river you will be safe,' Riana said.

As they started down the slope, a high-pitched beeping came from Paul's bumbag. He unzipped the bag and realised the sound was coming from the Eyestone. Riana stared at it, aghast. Before Paul could explain, the air was filled with a loud throbbing sound.

'Spellbinders!' Riana cried, looking up.

Paul followed her gaze and saw a large dark shape appear in the sky above the trees. Paul stared in amazement at the strange insect-like craft. 'The Spellbinders can fly?'

A beam of light speared down from the flying ship, catching Paul and Riana like rabbits in a spotlight. Riana dropped to her knees, whimpering with terror. Paul stared fearfully up at the black shape, wondering where on earth he was.

Finding the Way Home

Paul and Riana cowered inside the cone of bright light, staring up at the Spellbinder flying ship. The air was filled with the beeping of the Eyestone in Paul's hand and the heavy throbbing of the ship as it started to descend towards them.

'We will be banished,' Riana whimpered.

'Riana, we have to run,' Paul yelled. He pulled Riana to her feet and dragged her towards the nearest trees.

Riana looked over her shoulder. 'They're coming after us!'

The flying ship moved over the trees, the light-beam stabbing down. Paul and Riana ran under the canopy of branches, dodging trees and rocks, but the ship followed them unerringly. Paul flattened himself against a tree and desperately started banging the

Eyestone against the trunk.

'What are you doing?' Riana panted.

'They're tracking the Eyestone. I'm trying to turn it off.' The Eyestone kept beeping.

'Throw it away!'

'No. You stay here. I'll try and lead them away.' Paul ran out from under the trees. The light-beam moved after him. He hurdled a fallen tree trunk and found himself at the top of a steep bank. The ground gave way and he tumbled downwards, rolling to a stop close to the river. The light moved relentlessly towards him.

A tree limb floated in the river against the bank. Paul wedged the beeping Eyestone into its branches, pushed the limb into the current and then dived under a bush. The light-beam swept across him and moved over the water. A bolt of energy seared down. The limb burst into flames and the beeping stopped.

The throbbing faded as the flying ship moved away. Paul whirled around at the sound of a snapping twig.

Riana was standing at the top of the bank.

'I thought you'd gone,' she said, scrambling down to join him.

'Where would I go? I don't know your world. I need you to take me back to where you found me.'

Riana shook her head. 'It's too dangerous being with you. I'll show you where to cross the river but then I must leave you.'

'Then what am I going to do?'

'You're clever. You'll think of something.' Riana walked away along the bank.

Paul went after her. 'If you don't help me, I'll follow you.' Riana kept walking. Paul stayed by her side. 'I mean it. Everywhere you go, I'll be there. How are you going to explain that?'

Riana pushed him away. 'You stole an Eyestone. You have broken the Spellbinders' law.'

'But I didn't know I was breaking it. I'm not from here, remember. I'm from the future.'

Riana backed away. 'You're mad.'

'No! I can prove it.' Paul unzipped his bumbag and took out the Walkman. 'I bet you don't have these in this time. Put them on. They won't hurt you.'

Riana nervously allowed Paul to place the headphones over her ears. When he switched the Walkman on, Riana's eyes went wide. She pulled the headphones off, staring at them in astonishment. 'What is this?'

'It's music from the twentieth century. By Chocolate Rapper. They're a band. Now do you believe me?'

Riana moved easily along the dark forest track. She was wearing the headphones and the Walkman was clipped to her belt. Her head nodded up and down in time to the music.

'Slow down, will you?' Paul yelled as he struggled to keep up.

Riana didn't answer. She pushed aside a low branch. It swung back, catching Paul in the chest and knocking him to the ground. Riana walked on a few more paces and then paused.

'Paul, the music has stopped.' She turned and saw Paul lying on his back. 'What are you doing?'

'I've got to rest,' Paul gasped.

'Already? We've only just started.'

'I've walked further today than I have in my

whole life.' Paul started to unlace one of his runners. Riana sat beside him.

'Don't you travel far in your world?'

'Yes, but I normally take a bus.'

'A bus?'

'Never mind, you wouldn't understand.' Paul got his runner off and began massaging his foot. He looked curiously at the runner's thick rubber sole. 'I wonder if these are what saved me from the Spellbinder,' he mused. 'Maybe she used some kind of electricity and the rubber soles insulated me.'

'What is electricity?'

'You wouldn't understand.'

'Stop telling me I wouldn't understand. I'm not stupid!'

Riana got to her feet and stalked off up the track.

Paul hobbled after her, carrying his shoe. 'Riana, I'm sorry. It's just that my world's so different from yours. I'm just too tired to explain everything. I don't think you're stupid.'

Riana stopped. 'We'll find somewhere to camp for the night. Come on.'

FINDING THE WAY HOME

She pushed into the undergrowth beside the track. Paul pulled on his shoe and struggled through the bushes after her. He found himself in a clearing where Riana was already gathering twigs for a fire.

'You light the fire,' Riana said. 'I'll get some bigger wood.' She took an oilskin package from her belt and tossed it to Paul.

Inside the package was a pile of sawdust, a piece of worn metal and a flint stone. Paul looked at them in bewilderment. 'What am I supposed to do with these?'

'You wouldn't understand.' Riana smiled and Paul laughed. Riana took the package back. 'If you can't start a fire, how do you cook?'

'I use a microwave oven. But microwaves won't be invented for about a thousand years.'

Riana poured a little pile of sawdust onto the ground. She grasped the metal and struck the flint against it. A spark dropped into the sawdust. Riana blew gently and a wisp of smoke appeared as the sawdust started to smoulder. Riana placed some twigs over the sawdust, blew again and in a moment they caught fire.

Soon the campfire was blazing and Riana was cooking a meal in a small pot. She noticed Paul staring up at the sky and frowning. 'What's the matter?' she asked.

'If I've gone back in time, how can the Spellbinders have flying machines? What makes them fly?'

'Magic,' Riana whispered.

Paul snorted. 'There's no such thing as magic.'

Riana lifted the pot off the fire and poured some of the contents into a carved wooden bowl. 'Eat. It will make you feel better.'

Paul cautiously sniffed the steaming bowl. 'What is it?'

'Dried eel, root vegetables and wild herbs.'

Paul reared back in disgust. 'Gross!'

'That's all there is.' Riana scooped up some of the stew and ate hungrily.

Paul cautiously took a mouthful. Then he laughed. 'I must be dreaming. I mean, look what's happened to me. I've seen mutants, been zapped by a Spellbinder, chased by an angry mob and I haven't even got a scratch! And now I'm out in the forest with a pretty girl, eating dried eel and enjoying it. This has to be a dream.'

'If you're dreaming, who am I?' Riana asked.

'A figment of my imagination. Look, I'll prove it. Punch me. As hard as you can.'

Riana punched Paul in the arm.

'Ow! Alright. So it's not a dream. But I wish it was.'

When Paul had finished eating, he pulled the cloak around him and lay on his back. Countless stars blazed in the clear, unpolluted sky. 'I've never seen so many stars. Do you have names for the constellations?' He pointed upwards. 'That's the Southern Cross ... Wait a minute, you can't see that in the northern hemisphere. I can't be in England. I must still be in Australia.'

Paul sat up and looked excitedly at Riana. 'And there was an eclipse yesterday! It must still be the same year. I haven't gone back in time at all.'

Riana stared at him. 'I don't understand.'

'Neither do I. But somehow I'm in the same country and the same time but everything's different.'

'How are you going to return to your world?'

'I don't know. I have to get back to the place where I arrived in this one.'

'Where was that?'

'There was this weird-looking tower on top of a mountain near where I met you yesterday.'

A look of fear crossed Riana's face. 'That is the Summoning Tower of my village. It is forbidden to go there.'

'Look, just get me close and I'll take my chances.'

Riana shook her head. Paul picked up his Walkman. 'If you take me, I'll let you keep this.'

Riana hesitated for a moment, then held out her hand. Paul gave her the player. Riana smiled and put on the headphones.

Paul and Riana were cloaked in early morning mist as they climbed a steep narrow track. After spending a night on the ground huddled under his cloak, Paul was stiff and sore. He remembered his comfortable bed back home and prayed that he'd be in it that night.

Paul bumped into Riana as she stopped suddenly on the trail ahead of him. Painted on the rocks on either side of the trail were two of the snake signs.

'What are those?' Paul asked.

'Spellbinder signs. They mean that it is forbidden to go any further.'

'Why?'

'We do not ask such questions,' Riana said firmly. 'That's only for the Spellbinders to know.'

'But aren't you even curious? Don't you want to know?'

'I know enough to live my life. Why should I want to know anything else?'

'Because if you don't learn, you can't understand how the world works. You can't control your life.'

'The Spellbinders control my life.'

'Don't you care about that?'

'Why should I? I'm happy.'

Riana leaped onto the rock, climbed around the sign and dropped to the track on the other side.

'Why did you do that?' Paul asked.

Riana grinned. 'If we get caught, we won't have to lie about passing the sign.'

Paul laughed at Riana's ingenuity and did the same.

The track opened out into a clearing in which stood the massive Summoning Tower. Paul stared up at the tall framework of old rusting iron. Two huge arms reached out from either side of the hexagonal tower, forming a platform with the top. Around the base were rows of what looked like electrical insulators. Wondering what the tower was for, Paul desperately searched the area for a way home.

'Paul, hide!' Riana suddenly called.

They took cover behind a rocky outcrop just as the black-hatted Summoner appeared, accompanied by a man carrying a heavy wooden staff. The man stayed by the track, nervously keeping watch, as the Summoner approached the tower.

Paul watched as the Summoner placed an Eyestone in the metal dish that stood near the base of the tower. The dish was connected to the tower by thick metal cables. The Summoner opened the Eyestone. Power crackled along the cables and around the top of the tower.

'Spellbinders,' the Summoner called into the Eyestone, 'this is the Summoner of Clayhill.'

'Spellbinder Ashka hears you, Summoner,' a woman's voice crackled from the Eyestone. Paul recognised the voice of the Spellbinder from the market. 'Two of my villagers were attacked by Marauders yesterday,' the Summoner told her.

There was a loud snap of electricity and a bolt of power arced from the tower to the Eyestone.

'Spellbinder, something strange is happening,' the Summoner shouted.

Ashka's reply was lost in static as sparks flashed in front of the tower, creating a rippling curtain of energy. There was a tearing sound, and a rip appeared in the air.

'That's what happened before,' Paul excitedly told Riana. 'Maybe I can get back through!'

He started to move but Riana held him back. 'Wait!'

Riana darted to another outcrop and whirled her bolas. The Summoner ducked as they whizzed over his head.

'Marauders!' the Summoner yelled, pointing to where Riana was hiding.

The man with the staff came running but Riana was already racing through the rocks away from the tower. The man and the Summoner chased after her.

Paul ran towards the tower.

The snarl of a chainsaw echoed around the hillside. Alex and Katrina watched as a police officer cut through the branch holding up the cable running to the cave. Energy began crackling around the power lines above the tree.

'Look out!' Brian called.

Electricity leaped from the power lines and surged down the cable towards the cave where Alex and Katrina were standing.

'Get away from the cable!' the officer yelled.

As Paul ran towards the tower, the rip in the curtain of energy widened. Through it, he could see Alex and Katrina running from the cable. Then he saw Brian.

'Dad!' he shouted.

The faint sound of Paul's voice made Katrina look back. Through the curtain of energy, she saw Paul running towards her. 'Alex, look,' she yelled above the sound of the chainsaw.

Alex turned. At the same moment, the police officer severed the branch and the cable dropped. Sparks flew as it touched the ground and the rip in the air began to close.

'No, stop!' Paul yelled as he saw his way home disappearing. He put on a final burst of speed, but the doorway vanished just as he reached it. Paul stopped and looked around in despair. His way home was gone.

'I saw Paul!' Katrina yelled. She pointed to the cave. Brian, the police officer and Ms Gibson rushed over. 'I saw this sort of pulsing energy and Paul was on the other side of it.'

Everyone looked, but there was no sign of Paul.

'You're not helping Paul by making up more stories,' the policeman said.

'I'm not making up stories,' Katrina protested. 'I saw him. He was running towards me. Alex saw him too.'

The adults looked at Alex.

'Sorry, Mr Reynolds,' Alex said. 'I didn't see anything.'

Katrina stared at Alex in dismay.

'Katrina, it's been a long day,' Ms Gibson said. 'You must be tired.'

'I'm not tired,' Katrina snapped. 'I saw Paul! Why won't you believe me?'

Ms Gibson put her arm around Katrina. 'The poor girl's exhausted. Come on, we'll get you home.'

Choking back tears of frustration, Katrina allowed herself to be led away.

Paul stared in dismay at the place where the doorway had been. How was he going to get home now?

The sound of the Summoner's voice made him look up. 'Riana, you know it is forbidden to be here. What were you doing?'

Paul threw himself behind some rocks as the Summoner and his man appeared with Riana.

'I was hunting a deer last night and it led me here,' Riana lied. 'I didn't realise where I was.' She looked anxiously around and was relieved to see that Paul had gone.

The Summoner picked up the bolas. 'Are these yours?'

'Yes. I nearly hit the deer.'

'You nearly hit me!'

Riana bowed her head. 'Summoner, forgive me.'

'Don't let me find you here again,' the

Summoner said sternly and handed back her bolas.

'I won't, Summoner. I promise.'

Riana hurried away from the tower and down the track. As she passed the Spellbinder signs, Paul stuck his head up from behind a rock. 'Riana?'

Riana looked at Paul in surprise. 'I thought you went home?'

'The opening's gone. The cable Alex and I rigged at the cave somehow connected the power lines in my world to your Summoning Tower. That's how I got here. But now they've pulled the cable down, I'm stuck here forever.' Paul fought to hold back his panic. 'I saw my father there, Riana. I'll never see him again. What am I going to do?' He slumped against a rock and began to sob.

'Come with me,' Riana said gently. 'I'll ask my parents to help.'

Paul wiped his eyes and managed a smile. 'Thanks, Riana.' He shouldered his pack and followed her down the trail away from the

tower.

It was early afternoon when Riana and Paul emerged from the forest.

'Welcome to Clayhill,' Riana said.

Before them was a small village of neat thatched cottages, built along a narrow road and surrounded by wheat-fields. People were using hand tools to harvest the crop. A waterwheel turned in the stream beside a large barn. To Paul, the village looked like something out of a fairytale.

'Your TV sets must all have indoor aerials,' he said wryly.

Riana stared at him.

'Just a joke,' Paul explained. 'I meant that your life here is pretty simple compared to what I'm used to.'

'If you think I'm simple, you don't have to come with me,' Riana said indignantly. 'You can go back into the forest and try to survive on your own. But as you can't light a fire and you can't find food, I don't think you'll last very long.'

'Sorry, I wasn't being rude. I'm still getting used to the idea that I'm stuck here.'

Riana pointed to a group of men patrolling

the hillside above the village. 'They must be keeping watch for Marauders. We'll have to go carefully. We're not used to strangers here.'

Keeping low, Riana and Paul crept through the wheat to the stream. Sheltered by the bank, they made their way to the village barn and slipped through the open doorway.

The interior of the barn was cool and dim. Paul's nose wrinkled as he caught the smells of hay, grain and manure. Hoes, rakes and spades, all made of wood, hung from the walls.

'Until my parents agree to help, you must not be seen,' Riana said, leading the way up a wide ramp. At the top of the ramp, bales of hay were stacked around the walls.

Paul sniffed and made a face. 'Phew! What's that stink?'

Riana pointed to a rack. 'I'm curing rabbit skins,' Riana said proudly.

'I don't think the cure's working,' Paul joked.

Riana didn't laugh.

'Just stay out of sight until I get back,' she said curtly and disappeared down the ramp.

Riana opened the door of her cottage. Her six-year-old brother Jal's face lit up when he saw her. 'Riana's back!'

Riana's sister Arla ran to the door and hugged her. Arla was an almost identical but smaller version of Riana. 'Where have you been?' she asked. 'Da was attacked by Marauders.'

'They didn't scare me,' the thickset man beside the fire pit scoffed. 'I stood my ground and faced them fearlessly.'

Riana hurried over to where her father, Bron, was sitting. Her mother, Maran, was bandaging his swollen leg, her usually smiling face lined with concern.

'The Summoner has ordered lookouts to keep watch,' Maran told Riana. 'Anything strange is to be reported to him at once. Why were you so long in getting back? We thought you might have been hurt.'

Riana decided this wasn't the right moment to tell her parents about Paul. 'I saw Marauders too,' she answered. 'I had to hide while they passed. Then I took the long way home. Let me show you what I got at the market.'

Paul was lying behind a bale of hay, dozing in the heat of the afternoon sun when he heard someone coming up the ramp.

'Paul?' Riana called softly.

Paul sat up. Riana put an apple and some meat and bread on the bale. Paul snatched up the apple and bit into it hungrily.

'So when do I meet your parents?' Paul said, juice running down his chin.

'I didn't tell them.'

'Why?'

'I couldn't. It's too dangerous now. In a few days, things will quiet down and then I'll tell them.'

'What do I do till then?'

'I know a place in the forest you can hide.'

As Riana picked up Paul's pack, it fell open and the video-camera dropped out. Paul caught it. 'Careful! That's the most advanced piece of technology in this whole world.'

'What's it for?'

'It's a camera. It records pictures of things on this tape.' Paul touched a button on the camera and the tape popped out. He grinned excitedly. 'I can show you what my world is like. Look.'

As Paul put the videotape back in the camera, Jal crept to the top of the ramp. When he saw Riana with the stranger, he hid behind a pole. Paul held the camera out to Riana.

'There are tiny people in there,' Riana gasped as she watched the screen on the back.

The thought of tiny people in a box was strange, and any strange things were to be reported. Jal stole back down the ramp and raced out of the barn.

'The people aren't in there,' Paul explained to Riana. 'It's just a picture. A moving picture. That's my father.'

Riana peered at the tiny figures. 'What's his name?'

'Brian Reynolds. And that's my sister, Christine.'

Paul's face suddenly fell. 'They must think I'm dead by now.'

'We'd better go,' Riana said.

Paul put the camera back in his pack, pulled on his cloak and followed Riana down the ramp. As they headed for the door, it was thrown open and Bron and Maran appeared.

'Riana, get away from him!' Maran ordered.

'But, Ma ...'

'Do as I say.' Riana reluctantly moved away from Paul.

Maran looked at him warily. 'Who are you?'

'His name is Paul,' Riana answered. 'I met him on the road.'

'Where are you from?' Bron asked.

'He's from the north,' Riana said quickly. 'The far north.'

'What's the name of your village?'

'Sydney,' Paul replied.

'I've never heard of it,' Maran said suspiciously.

'It's very small,' Paul explained. 'Way out in the sticks. It doesn't even have a postcode.'

'A what?' Bron asked.

'Da, Paul saved my life,' Riana said. 'I fell in the river and he pulled me out. I would have drowned. Can he stay with us for a while?'

'No,' Maran said vehemently. 'He could be a Marauder.'

Bron laughed. 'Nonsense. I've seen Marauders. He doesn't look anything like them.'

'Well, I don't want strangers in my house.

You heard what the Summoner said. We must report him.'

'Please, Ma,' Riana pleaded. 'He could take over for Da in the fields.'

'Who is this?' a voice boomed.

Everyone looked round. The Summoner was standing in the doorway, his eyes fixed on Paul.

It Isn't Magic, It's Science

Riana and her parents watched fearfully as the Summoner walked into the barn. He was the Spellbinders' voice in Clayhill and his word was law. He stared suspiciously at Paul.

'His name is Paul,' Riana said quickly. 'He's ... my cousin.'

Bron put his arm around Paul's shoulders. 'That's right. Haven't seen him for years.'

The Summoner nodded, satisfied by the explanation. 'How long will you be staying in Clayhill, Paul?'

Paul stole a look at Maran and Bron. 'I'm not sure.'

'Don't worry, Summoner,' Bron promised. 'He'll be out in the fields tomorrow with the rest of us.'

'Enjoy your stay.'

The Summoner took a string of onions from

the barn wall and left.

Maran glared angrily at Bron. 'You lied to the Summoner!'

Bron shrugged. 'What else could I do? Riana brought the boy here. Do you want her banished?'

'We don't know where he's from,' Maran protested.

'What does it matter? He saved our daughter's life.'

'Can Paul stay?' Riana begged. 'Please?'

Maran stared disdainfully at Paul. 'He sleeps in the barn.' She stalked out.

'It could have been worse,' Bron said to Paul. 'She could have made you sleep with the pigs.'

Paul smiled wanly. He'd had warmer welcomes.

Katrina sat at the dinner table with her mother and father, but her mind wasn't on her food. As she fiddled with her mashed potatoes, she remembered Paul trying to get through the weird rippling energy at the cave, trying to escape from wherever he was. But where was that?

'I know you're upset, sweetheart,' Mrs Muggleton was saying. 'But you should try to eat something. I'm sure the police will find Paul.'

Katrina knew there was no point in arguing and started to eat.

'What I want to know,' Mr Muggleton said, 'is why you were up at that cave at night anyway. Was something going on with you and one of those boys?'

Katrina was outraged. 'No! Lisa and I were trying to get a photo of a ghost.'

'A ghost?' her father scoffed. 'There's no such thing.'

'I know that, Dad. But something weird happened up there.'

'Katrina, don't start that again. People don't just vanish.' Mr Muggleton slammed his knife and fork down on his plate.

'Now, Scott,' Mrs Muggleton said patiently. 'there are many things in this world we don't

understand. My astrologer's been to the

Bermuda Triangle and she says it could be the doorway to another dimension.'

Katrina's father groaned. He didn't think much of astrology. Katrina didn't either but she had heard of the Bermuda Triangle. Ships and planes disappeared there. Maybe something similar had happened to Paul.

'What's a dimension?' she asked.

'See?' Mr Muggleton said. 'The girl's taking you seriously. Stop filling her head with nonsense.'

'It's not nonsense,' Mrs Muggleton argued. 'My aromatherapist thinks ...'

'Beverly!'

Mrs Muggleton turned to Katrina. 'Could you manage some ice cream, dear?'

Katrina nodded. She would solve this problem herself. And quickly. Paul's life might depend upon it.

A hand grasped Paul's shoulder and shook him.

'I'm tired, Dad.' Paul murmured. 'Let me go back to sleep.'

'Paul, it's Riana. It's time for work.'

Paul awoke, remembering with a jolt of dismay where he was. Riana was standing over him, holding a lantern.

Paul peered between the slats in the barn wall. 'It's still dark.'

'By the time you dress and have breakfast, it won't be,' Riana said. 'Get up. Everyone who eats must work. It is the law.'

Paul threw off the skins he had been sleeping under. He was only wearing his Garfield print jockettes. Riana stared at the orange cat on his underwear and Paul quickly pulled the skins back.

Riana smiled at his embarrassment. 'I'd better find you some other clothes.'

A short time later, dressed in homespun clothes and leather boots, Paul walked with Riana and her family towards a field. They all carried wooden hoes and spades. The sun was just over the horizon but other villagers were already in the field, preparing it for planting. Paul realised that all of their tools were made of wood. There were no metal implements anywhere. And no machines.

Everything was done by hand.

As Riana's family approached, the villagers stared at Paul.

'Our people are suspicious of anything different,' Riana warned him. 'Don't talk. Just do whatever you're told.'

Paul grimaced. 'Sounds just like school.'

Riana stopped at an untilled piece of ground and started to hoe it. Paul lifted his spade uncertainly.

'Have you ever used a spade?' Riana asked.

'I think I can figure it out.' He could use a computer. Any fool could handle a spade. He plunged it deeply into the earth and pulled back hard on the handle. It snapped, sending Paul sprawling on his back. The villagers laughed.

'Where's this nephew of yours from, Bron?' one asked. 'He can't even use a spade.'

Paul got to his feet, feeling very foolish.

'I'm going to take Paul to the top field and start planting the beans,' Riana told Bron. 'Jal, get a bucket and carry water for us.'

'A plough would make this work so much easier,' Paul said as Riana led him away. 'One man could do all these fields in a day. I could help you build one.'

'We can only use tools that the Spellbinders give us,' Riana explained.

'Why?'

'It is the law.'

'That's stupid. Why?'

'I don't know,' Riana admitted, unsettled by Paul's questions.

Sweat poured down Paul's face as he pushed holes in the ground with a pointed stick. Riana followed him, dropping a seed into each hole. Jal came after them, watering the seeds from a bucket before covering them with earth. Paul stopped to straighten his aching back. There had to be a better way of doing this.

An hour later, Paul was grinning as he clumped awkwardly across the field. Tied to the soles of his boots were pieces of wood with short, sharpened sticks poking out of them: each time Paul lifted a foot, he left a row of holes in the ground.

'This is a much easier way to do the work,' Riana chirped, rolling seeds into the holes down a hollow reed.

Jal held another hollow reed full of water,

his thumb held tightly over the upper end. He released his thumb and water flowed into the holes. 'What magic did you use to keep the water in the reed?' he asked Paul.

Paul chuckled. 'It's not magic. It's just air pressure.'

'Whatever it is, we must be careful no-one sees us,' Riana warned.

In the lower fields, a group of children started yelling, 'Gryvon is coming! Gryvon is coming!'

Everyone stopped work to watch Gryvon, the Spellbinder Ashka's Apprentice, riding into Clayhill. The sharp-featured youth was the son of the village Summoner, and the people of Clayhill were proud that one of them was destined to become a Spellbinder.

'Doesn't he look handsome?' Maran asked Bron as she admired Gryvon's well-cut blue and grey uniform.

'I hope the Spellbinders have taught him some manners,' Bron replied.

'Bron!' Maran feared that one day her husband's lack of respect for the Spellbinders would get him into trouble.

Gryvon stopped outside the Summoner's cottage and dismounted. The Summoner came out and hugged him.

'What brings you home, my son?' he asked.

'Ashka is worried about all the Marauders that have been seen in this area. She wants me to investigate.'

'Good. Let me take care of your horse.'

As his father led the horse towards the barn, Gryvon noticed Jal by the creek, filling his bucket with water.

'Hello, Jal,' he called. 'Where's that pretty sister of yours?'

Jal stared in awe at the Apprentice.

'Don't be afraid,' Gryvon said. 'I'm not a Spellbinder yet. Would you like a sweetcake?'

He held out the honey-flavoured treat. 'Tell me where Riana is.'

Jal pointed up the hill. Gryvon tossed the sweetcake but the throw was wide and it fell into the deep water. Jal wondered how he was going to get it.

'We don't have to walk everywhere,' Paul told Riana as they continued planting. 'We have cars—they're a kind of chair with wheels. You sit in the chair and it takes you wherever you want to go.'

'Could this chair take me to Rivertown?' Riana asked, amazed at the idea.

'Well, no, you don't have any roads.'

'Could it take me up the river?'

'No.'

'Could it take me across the fields?'

'Not without destroying your crops,' Paul chuckled.

'Then these chairs would be no use in our world,' Riana said.

'OK,' Paul conceded. 'But the point is, let's say you wanted a chair—I mean, a car. The Spellbinders should let you have one.'

'So the Spellbinders are wrong for not letting us have something for which we have no use?'

Paul shook his head in exasperation and continued to march across the field in his planting boots.

'It is forbidden to sow fields like that!' a voice bellowed. Paul and Riana looked around and saw Gryvon. Riana quickly bowed her head. Gryvon stared suspiciously at the contraptions on Paul's feet and then at Paul. 'Who are you?' he demanded.

Riana kicked Paul in the ankle. 'This is my cousin Paul, Apprentice.'

Paul quickly bowed, hoping that Gryvon wouldn't recognise him from the market town.

'Where are you from?' Gryvon asked.

Before Paul could answer, a woman screamed from the village, 'Bron! It's your son! Hurry!'

Riana ran towards the creek. Gryvon went after her. Paul tried to follow but tripped over the wood attached to his boots. He hurriedly began unlacing them.

By the time Paul arrived, the whole village was silently watching Bron climb from the creek carrying Jal's limp body. Riana was trying to comfort her mother and sister. Bron carefully lay Jal on the ground. An elderly woman pushed her way through the crowd. She was the village Healer. She knelt beside Jal and put her ear to his mouth.

'There's no breath,' the Healer announced. 'I'm sorry, Bron.'

Bron cried out in anguish.

Paul pushed forward. 'Maybe I can start him breathing again.'

Maran stood in his path. 'Stay away from my son!'

'Please,' Paul pleaded. 'The longer we wait, the less chance there is of saving him.'

'Ma,' Riana implored, 'if Jal is dead then Paul can't do him any more harm.'

Bron looked down at Jal's lifeless body. 'Let him try, Maran.'

Maran stepped aside. Paul quickly knelt beside Jal and began giving him mouth-to-mouth resuscitation. The villagers watched in astonishment as Jal's chest began to rise and fall. Paul felt for a pulse in Jal's neck—but could feel nothing.

'His heart's stopped,' he told Riana. 'Help me.'

Riana knelt uncertainly beside Jal.

'When I tell you, hold his nose and blow air into his mouth.'

Paul pressed rapidly on Jal's chest five times. 'Now Riana, two breaths. Watch his chest rise.'

Riana blew into Jal's mouth. Paul felt Jal's neck. There was still no pulse. Paul pressed down again on Jal's chest and the boy suddenly coughed. The villagers stared in wonder as Jal's eyes opened. Maran hugged Bron with joy. Paul smiled at Riana with relief.

Paul sat with Riana's family around the table eating lunch. Jal lay on the couch under a blanket, sipping broth.

'I'm going to set up a bed for you in here,' Bron said to Paul. 'It's far too draughty in that barn.' Maran nodded her agreement.

Riana smiled at Paul. 'Now you can stay here for as long as you want.'

Paul tried to look grateful. What he really wanted was to get home to his own family.

There was a knock at the door. Riana got up to open it and was not pleased to see Gryvon outside. Everyone stood to bow. Paul reluctantly followed their lead.

'I came to see how Jal is,' Gryvon said, coming in.

'I'm alright,' Jal said from the couch. 'Thanks to Paul.'

Gryvon looked at Paul. 'How did you bring the boy back to life?'

'My father taught me,' Paul said. 'He's a scient ... a healer.'

'You didn't tell me what village you are from.'

'Sydney,' Paul and Riana replied together.

'I've flown all over this land,' Gryvon declared, 'and I've never heard of it.'

'You've been in a flying ship?' Arla asked, her eyes wide with wonder.

'I've flown to the end of the world,' Gryvon boasted, 'and looked over the edge.'

Paul started to laugh.

'Time to go back to work,' Riana said. 'Excuse us, Apprentice.' She dragged Paul out of the door.

'Gryvon's a liar,' Paul told Riana as they trudged away from the cottage. 'The world doesn't have an edge. It's round, like a ball. And people live all over it.'

Riana looked at Paul as if he was mad. 'But they'd fall off the bottom into the fire.'

'There's no fire under the world!'

Riana pointed to the sun. 'Every day the sun dies and every night it passes through the fires beneath the world so that in the morning it will be full of heat again.'

Paul was incredulous. 'Riana, the sun never goes out. The world just rotates so that we face away from it. The sun doesn't go around the world, OK? The world goes around the sun.'

Riana looked bewildered.

'Look, you be the sun. I'm the world.' He circled slowly around Riana, keeping his face towards her: 'Now it's day.' Then still circling, he turned away from her: 'Now it's night.' Paul continued his demonstration as Riana struggled to understand this startling new concept.

'What are they doing?' Gryvon asked as he and Bron watched Paul's antics from the cottage door.

'Paul must be teaching Riana a dance from his village.'

Gryvon shook his head. 'It's a very strange dance.'

'Blight!' a woman suddenly cried from the fields. 'There's red blight on the wheat!'

She ran up to Bron and Gryvon, holding a sheaf of wheat stalks. They were covered in dark red spots.

'The blight must be stopped before it spreads to the other fields,' Bron said and hurried away to tell the Summoner.

After the day's work was over, Riana and Paul washed off in a swimming hole under a waterfall. They stretched out to dry on a warm rock beside the water. Riana took out the Walkman and put on the headphones. She pressed a button, expecting to hear music, but her eyes opened wide with fear and she pulled off the headphones. 'Paul, listen!'

Paul put the headphones on and was surprised to hear the Summoner's worried voice: 'The red blight threatens our crops. Spellbinder, I ask that you help us.'

Ashka answered him. 'Tell your people to stay in their homes tonight. We will cast a powerful spell.'

There was silence.

'You turned the radio on by mistake,' Paul excitedly told Riana. 'The Eyestones must be radios. And the Summoning Tower must be a broadcasting tower.'

Riana stared at him. 'I don't understand.'

'We've got to go to the field tonight and see this magic spell,' Paul said. 'I'm starting to see through these Spellbinders.'

Once everyone was asleep, Paul and Riana sneaked out of the cottage. As they made their way through the deserted village, a faint, familiar throbbing could be heard in the distance. A dark shape appeared in the sky over the hills.

Riana pulled Paul under some trees as the Spellbinder flying ship swooped over the fields. It trailed a fine mist which covered the wheat. Paul caught some on his hand. He sniffed it and recognised the smell of chemicals. 'The Spellbinders are crop-dusting!' he realised in amazement.

Riana just looked confused.

'They're spraying the fields with poisons to kill the blight. The Spellbinders aren't magicians. They use science, just like in my world.'

Paul watched the flying ship disappear into the night. 'Where do they come from?'

'A castle to the west of the great forest,'

Riana said. 'Its towers are so high, they touch the clouds.'

'Have you been there?'

'No, it is forbidden. But Gryvon says it's the most beautiful place you can imagine.'

Paul was suddenly filled with hope. 'Maybe the Spellbinders can help me get home.'

In the morning, Paul and Riana went to the Summoner's cottage. Gryvon was outside, grooming his horse.

'Gryvon, can I talk to you?' Paul asked respectfully.

Gryvon dipped his brush in a bucket of soapy water and kept working. 'My correct title is Apprentice.'

'Right. Apprentice. Sorry,' Paul said. 'Listen, I need to get to the castle and speak with the Spellbinders.'

Gryvon stared at Paul. 'Are you mad? You know that is forbidden.'

'I need the Spellbinders' help to get home,' Paul explained. 'I know this'll be hard to believe and I don't understand how it happened but ... I come from another world.'

'Your cousin has been out in the sun too long,' Gryvon said sarcastically to Riana.

Paul wished he'd brought the video-camera. 'Come to the barn. I can prove it.' He grabbed Gryvon's arm.

'No, Paul!' Riana warned.

Gryvon threw off Paul's hand. 'You dare to touch an Apprentice? Apologise!'

'I'm sorry,' Paul stammered. 'But ...'

Gryvon cut him off. 'Properly. On your knees.'

'What?'

'Get down on your knees and apologise for touching me.'

'Do it, Paul,' Riana said. 'Touching an Apprentice is forbidden. It is the law.'

Paul reluctantly knelt in front of Gryvon.

'Apprentice Gryvon,' he said mechanically, 'I'm sorry for touching you.'

Gryvon hurled the bucket of water over Paul. 'Keep your crazy cousin away from me,' he said to Riana. 'And be thankful I was lenient.' He went back to his grooming.

Riana led the wet and angry Paul away.

'Cheer up,' she said to Paul. 'We'll think of a way to make Gryvon believe you.'

'How?' Paul asked hopelessly. 'He's a total idiot. If brains were gunpowder, he couldn't even blow his nose.'

They made their way dejectedly back to Riana's cottage where they found the Healer examining Bron's injured leg. As she pulled away the bloodied dressing, Bron roared with pain and kicked over the stool on which sat the Healer's herbs and powders. A bottle rolled into the fireplace, spilling yellow powder which erupted into a cloud of foul-smelling smoke.

Paul pulled the bottle out of the flames. There was a label on it but he couldn't read the strange writing. 'What is this?' he asked the Healer.

'We use it for stopping infections. It's called goodyellow.'

Paul sniffed the bottle. 'Where I come from, it's called sulphur.'

That gave Paul an idea. 'I just thought of a way to blow Gryvon's nose,' he whispered excitedly to Riana, pocketing the bottle.

'Why are we here?' Riana asked nervously as she led Paul once more up the track towards the Summoning Tower.

'I think this world exists parallel to mine,' Paul tried to explain. 'So maybe the things that occur naturally in my world are also in yours.'

Paul went into the cave behind the tower and shone his torch on the roof. The beam illuminated some white crystals. 'Bingo,' he exclaimed. 'Saltpetre.' He began using a knife to scrape the crystals into a bag.

Riana rubbed a finger over the crystals then put it in her mouth, grimacing at the bitter taste. 'What do you want with the bittercrystal?'

Paul grinned. 'I'm planning a little surprise for Gryvon.'

In the barn, Arla and Jal peered curiously at Paul's video-camera. 'Riana said there were tiny people in it,' Jal told his sister.

As Arla examined the camera, she accidentally pressed the eject button and the videotape dropped out. Arla picked it up and tried to see if the tiny people were inside.

They looked up guiltily as Riana and Paul came into the barn. Paul had the bag of saltpetre and Riana carried a bucket. Jal quickly put the camera back in Paul's pack. Riana saw him.

'Jal,' she snapped, 'leave Paul's things alone.' Arla stuffed the videotape under her tunic and ran out of the barn with Jal.

Paul put a pottery bowl on a bench and poured some saltpetre into it.

'Tell me what you're doing,' Riana asked.

'Making gunpowder. Hand me the charcoal.'

Riana gave Paul the bucket. He put a handful of charcoal into the bowl and then took the Healer's bottle from his pocket. Uncorking it, he carefully poured some of the yellow powder into the bowl. He began crushing the mixture with a stick.

'What is gunpowder for?'

'Fireworks.'

'What do fireworks do?'

Paul took a pinch of the mixture from the bowl and sprinkled it into the flame of a lamp. The gunpowder flared brightly.

'Magic!' Riana whispered.

'No,' Paul said firmly. 'Science.'

Katrina walked along the school library aisle, reading a book. She was so engrossed that she didn't see Ms Gibson and bumped into her. The book fell to the floor and Ms Gibson picked it up.

'*Secrets of the Bermuda Triangle*,' she read. 'I didn't know you were into science fiction.' She handed back the book.

'Ms Gibson,' Katrina asked, 'do you believe that there are other places ... other worlds that we don't know about?'

'Like other planets?'

'No. Other ... dimensions.'

'Well, quantum physicists are making some pretty amazing discoveries,' Ms Gibson said. 'They have a theory that there may be other worlds which exist parallel to ours.'

Katrina knew she'd hit paydirt. 'Can you explain it to me?' she asked.

Ms Gibson chuckled. 'Not in a lunchtime.'

She looked over the shelves of books and pulled one out. It was titled *An Introduction to Quantum Physics*. 'This should give you the basic theory,' she said, handing it to Katrina. 'If you have any questions, come and ask me. But I can't guarantee I'll be able to answer them.'

Katrina smiled. 'Thanks, miss.' She sat down with the book and eagerly started to read.

It was evening and the inside of the barn was dark. Riana held a lamp as Paul put the completed fireworks into his pack. They were small clay pots, filled with gunpowder and sealed with wax. 'Let's go and surprise Gryvon,' Paul said.

Suddenly, they heard shouts and screams of fear from outside. Riana raced through the door. Paul grabbed his pack and the lamp and went after her.

Outside the barn, frightened villagers were running past. 'Marauders are attacking the village!' one yelled. 'Run!'

'They're stealing the Spellbinders' tribute,' another frightened voice called from the darkness.

Paul and Riana raced into the village square. While a group of hideous Marauders chased screaming villagers into the fields, others were stealing sacks of grain from the storehouse. One Marauder tore the Spellbinder sign off the roof and trampled it.

Gryvon and his father strode out of the Summoner's cottage.

'I am the Apprentice Gryvon,' Gryvon shouted. 'Leave Clayhill or suffer the wrath of the Spellbinders!'

Two Marauders moved towards them, whirling bullroarers. Behind them, Bron limped into the square, carrying a staff. 'Get away from them!' he yelled.

One of the Marauders whipped his bull-roarer around Bron's staff and pulled. Bron fell to the ground and the Marauder leaped on him. Without thinking, Riana raced across the square and leaped on the Marauder's back.

There was a loud blast from Paul's air-horn. The Marauder threw Riana off and turned to face Paul, who was holding a firework, its fuse burning. As the Marauder stepped towards him, Paul threw the firework at the Marauder's feet. The flame disappeared inside the clay pot but nothing happened.

The Marauder took another step towards Paul. Then the firework exploded between its legs. The Marauder cried out and staggered away.

The other Marauders dropped their sacks and moved towards Paul, who quickly lit more fireworks and tossed them. They exploded in balls of smoke and flame. The Marauders began to back away. Emboldened, other villagers appeared out of the darkness and started to advance on the Marauders. The Marauders fled, quickly vanishing among the trees.

The villagers gathered around Paul, staring at him with respect and awe.

'Did you see that?' Bron shouted. 'My nephew drove off the Marauders. Isn't he a marvel?'

Gryvon and the Summoner pushed through the crowd and confronted Paul. 'It is forbidden to use magic,' Gryvon said, trying to hide his fear. The boy had powers like the Spellbinders.

'That wasn't magic,' Riana corrected him. 'It's science.'

'I told you,' Paul said to Gryvon. 'I'm from another world. I can prove it.'

He opened his pack and took out the video-camera. The villagers stepped back fearfully.

'It won't hurt you,' Paul promised. 'It's a box that records pictures. I can show you what my world looks like.' He pushed the play button— but the screen stayed blank. He opened the camera and discovered that the videotape was missing. Paul desperately searched through his pack. 'There was a tape,' he told Gryvon. 'A black box. It must still be in the barn.'

Gryvon stared at Paul's pack. 'That bag was in Ashka's tent at Rivertown!'

The Summoner suddenly recognised Paul. 'You were the one who stole my Eyestone.' He turned to the villagers. 'Seize him! I'll summon the Spellbinders.'

Two villagers roughly grabbed Paul. Gryvon snatched the camera and pack.

'Paul saved the village,' Riana protested.

'You can't punish him for that.'

'The law is the law,' Gryvon said sternly.

'He didn't know,' Riana argued. 'He's from another ...'

'Riana,' Paul interrupted, 'shut up!'

'Lock him up!' Gryvon ordered.

Stung by Paul's words, Riana watched helplessly as Paul was dragged away and imprisoned in the storehouse.

Riana waited until everyone had returned to their homes, then crept silently through the shadows to the back of the storehouse. 'Paul,' she whispered through the bars, 'I've come to get you out.'

'No,' Paul whispered back. 'I don't want to get out. My plan worked. The Spellbinders are coming. They're my one chance to get home.'

Across the square, the door of the Summoner's cottage opened and Gryvon and his father came out.

'It's time,' the Summoner told the two men standing guard. They started to move towards the storehouse.

'Riana, if you want to help,' Paul said

107

quickly, 'find the videotape—the black box. The Spellbinders will want to see my world. It must be in the barn somewhere.'

Riana ducked out of sight as the guards opened the storehouse door. Without looking back, Paul stepped out. The guards grabbed his arms and followed Gryvon and the Summoner out of the village. Keeping the storehouse between herself and the guards, Riana ran back across the square.

As they approached the Summoning Tower, the throbbing of a flying ship could be heard. Paul grinned. Everything was going according to plan.

'Thanks for your hospitality, guys,' he said cheerily.

'You have no reason to smile,' the Summoner told him. 'You've broken the law.'

'Once I tell the Spellbinders where I'm from, they won't care.'

'The Spellbinders won't listen to you,' Gryvon said.

'Are you kidding? I'm from another world.'

'The Spellbinders won't care where you're

from,' Gryvon gloated. 'You'll be banished.'

'What do you mean?'

Gryvon hung the pack around Paul's neck. 'You'll be sent to the Wastelands. No-one ever comes back.'

The Summoner nodded to the guards, who prodded Paul towards the Summoning Tower with their staves.

The flying ship appeared over the hill and the throbbing became deafening. Electrical sparks leaped between the top of the tower and the bug-like craft as it descended. His jauntiness gone, Paul stared up in terror.

Secrets

'I'm from another world,' Paul screamed over the throbbing of the flying ship. 'You've got to believe me!'

Gryvon and the Summoner ignored his plea. There was a loud clang as the massive ship came to rest on the top of the Summoning Tower.

Riana peered out from behind a rock and saw the Summoner's men push Paul towards the tower. Paul was forced to climb the rusting ladder that ran up the centre of the tower. A circular hatch opened in the bottom of the ship. Trying to control his panic, Paul climbed towards it.

A muscular arm reached down and pulled Paul into the ship. Paul stared into the unfriendly face of a man in a black leather uniform. His head was shaved. The guard took

Paul's pack and pushed the frightened boy to the floor.

Paul looked around the interior of the ship. It was built from plates of corroded iron held together by rusting rivets. Sagging pipes and frayed cables ran across the walls and floor. The craft looked badly in need of repair.

'Don't send me to the Wastelands,' Paul begged. 'I didn't know I was breaking the law!'

'Silence!' the guard yelled.

'But I'm from another world.'

A padded leather seat in the nose of the ship swivelled round and the Spellbinder Ashka stared at Paul. 'I know you.'

'I was at Rivertown,' Paul replied. 'You thought I was a Marauder.'

'How did you escape my power-bolt?'

Paul pointed to his runners. 'The rubber soles insulated me.'

Ashka gestured and the guard brought Paul forward. Ashka inspected Paul's strange-looking shoes.

'I bet you've never seen anything like these before.' Paul pointed to his pack. 'I've got other things from my world in there.'

'Were you the one who drove off the Marauders at Clayhill?' Ashka asked.

'Yes. But I didn't know I was breaking the law. I was trying to help. Please don't send me to the Wastelands!'

'That's not my decision.'

Ashka swung the chair back to face the window in the nose of the ship. Paul watched as she checked the readings on a row of brass gauges. Ashka turned a control wheel, then released the lock on a long lever and slowly pulled it back. A block of glistening stone in the floor of the ship rotated. The throbbing sound increased and the ship started to vibrate. The guard pushed Paul into an uncomfortable metal seat.

Riana watched in dismay as the ship rose off the tower in a shower of sparks. It hovered in the air then turned to the west and flew over the hill. The throbbing sound faded.

Riana sneaked away from the tower and ran back to Clayhill. She met her father and mother crossing the square.

'Where have you been?' Bron asked angrily.

'To the Summoning Tower. Paul ...'

'You must forget Paul,' Maran snapped.

'But he saved our village,' Riana protested.

Maran shook her head. 'He broke the law.'

'Then the law is unfair!'

Maran and Bron were shocked by their daughter's outburst. Then Bron saw Gryvon and his father enter the square. He and Maran hurried Riana away before they were seen.

As the Summoner went towards his cottage, Gryvon noticed two of Paul's unexploded fireworks on the ground. He carefully picked them up.

'Where are you taking me?' Paul asked Ashka.

The Spellbinder's hands and feet were busy with the controls as she piloted the cumbersome flying ship through the night. Paul wondered what kept it in the air as it had no propulsion system he could see.

'You're going to the castle,' Ashka replied. 'The Regents will question you.'

'Who are the Regents?'

'Where did you say you're from?' Ashka asked incredulously.

'You're probably going to find this hard to believe, but I'm from another world.'

'I don't understand.'

'It's pretty hard to explain,' Paul admitted. 'I think your world and my world exist side by side. They're the same but different.'

'How can something be the same but different?'

Paul struggled to think of a metaphor. 'Imagine a line of red balloons, stretching out to infinity,' he said after a moment. 'Your universe is one balloon and mine is the one next to it.'

'What is a balloon?' Ashka asked.

Paul sighed. Getting the Spellbinders to believe his story was going to be harder than he'd thought.

Maran and Bron pushed Riana through the door of the cottage.

'You have to forget about Paul,' Bron said sternly. 'Think of what happened as a dream. And now you're awake.'

'It wasn't a dream,' Riana protested.

Arla and Jal looked down from the loft.

Riana saw Paul's videotape in Arla's hand. 'That's Paul's!' she exclaimed, grabbing the tape from Arla. 'Ma, Da, I have to go to the Spellbinders' castle. When they see the pictures on this, they'll believe Paul's story and help him get back to his world.'

'Stop this foolishness,' Maran cried. 'There is no other world.'

Riana pulled Paul's Walkman from her bag.

'What is it?' Bron asked, running his fingers over the unfamiliar smooth plastic case.

'It's from Paul's world. He calls it a Walkman. Listen.' Riana placed the headphones over her mother's ears and switched on the tape.

Maran ripped the headphones off. 'There was music in my head!'

'Now do you believe me? Paul needs my help. He saved my life and Jal's. I have to go.'

Riana went towards the door but Maran blocked her way. 'You're not going anywhere. Go to your bed. Your father and I will decide what to do.'

Riana looked pleadingly at her father but

Bron shook his head. Riana stormed to her bed.

The guard kept a wary eye as Paul examined the glistening stone in the ship's floor.

'This is what powers this ship, right?' Paul asked Ashka.

'We are Spellbinders,' she replied archly. 'Our powers are beyond your comprehension.'

Paul chuckled. 'Listen, you're not dealing with some dumb hick here. This is a scam, just like in *The Wizard of Oz*. You want everybody to think you're magicians but you're not. You're scientists. You're ...'

Paul stopped. In the distance, silhouetted against the rising sun, was a huge castle. Massive bolts of electricity crackled around a tall tower on its roof. Ashka pushed a lever forward and the flying ship began to descend.

Riana was in the barn, hurriedly filling her bag with supplies. She had to get out of the village before her parents realised she had gone. As she hung her favourite set of bolas from her belt, the barn door creaked. Riana whirled round and saw Bron in the doorway. 'You can't stop me going to the castle,' she said defiantly.

'You don't know the way.'

'I'll find it.' Riana turned away and took a coil of rope from the wall.

'You're as stubborn as your mother,' Bron said. 'Give me that.' He snatched the rope from Riana and tossed it away. Riana bristled with anger. Bron lifted a coil of new rope from the wall and held it out. 'Take this. It's strong. I wove it myself.' Riana took it and hugged her father.

'When you get to the castle,' Bron said, 'leave the black box at the gate and come straight home. Promise?'

Riana put the videotape in the top of her bag. 'I promise.' She kissed her father and hurried out of the barn.

With a shower of sparks, the flying ship touched down on a scarred metal platform in the castle courtyard. The guard pushed Paul out of the hatch. He looked up at the bolts of power crackling around the tower on the castle roof. 'You guys don't have electricity,' Paul said to Ashka as she came out of the ship. 'Where does all that power come from?'

Ashka didn't answer. She grabbed Paul's arm and hurried him into the castle. Paul stared up at the ornately carved vaulted ceilings as Ashka hustled him along a corridor. The massive building appeared ancient but was well maintained. Even at this early hour, servants in grey uniforms were mopping floors and dusting statues. They bowed their heads in silence as Ashka passed. Paul's mind was racing. Who had built this place? Where did the Spellbinders get their technology? Why did they pretend to be magicians?

There was the sound of voices. Ashka suddenly pulled Paul out of sight behind a pillar as two Spellbinders strolled past.

'Why all the secrecy?' Paul asked once they had gone.

Ashka ignored the question. She hurried Paul to a heavy wooden door and pushed him through.

The apartment inside was spacious and richly appointed. Ashka closed the door and bolted it. 'Show me the magic you used to defeat the Marauders,' she demanded.

'It wasn't magic,' Paul said. 'It was fire-works.'

'Fireworks?'

Paul picked up a small vase. 'You put gunpowder in this, stick in a fuse, seal the end and you've got a firework. Light the fuse and it goes bang.'

'How did you come by this knowledge?'

'I told you. I'm from another world.'

'Impossible.'

Paul opened his pack and took out the torch and the air-horn. 'Then where did these come from?' He switched on the torch and pointed it at Ashka. Dazzled by the beam, she backed away. 'It's just a torch. See?' Paul shone the beam on his hand, then handed the torch to the Spellbinder.

Fascinated, Ashka played the light over her hand. She looked shrewdly at Paul. Perhaps there was some truth in his story. If so, she could learn things from him that would give her an advantage over the other Spellbinders. She gave Paul a friendly smile.

There was a knock at the door. 'Ashka?'

Ashka quickly put the torch in the pack and pushed it under the bed. 'Hide that,' she hissed.

Paul shoved the air-horn down his pants as Ashka opened the door. A tall Spellbinder stood outside. 'The Regents are waiting,' she told Ashka.

'I'm coming now,' said Ashka, and the tall Spellbinder left.

Ashka led Paul out of the apartment. Closing the door, she turned to him and spoke in a low voice. 'You are in great danger. If the Regents decide you have broken the law, they will banish you. I shall try to save you but you must say nothing. You must let me speak.'

Paul nodded. He didn't know if he could trust Ashka but he had no choice. All he wanted was to get home.

Two guards held the doors open while Ashka led Paul into the Regents' chamber. It was a long room with high windows overlooking the castle courtyard. At one end, three ornately carved chairs stood behind a heavy wooden table. Regent Lukan, a bearded middle-aged man, sat in the centre chair. Regent Marna, a younger woman with long dark hair, sat on his left. The third chair was empty. Both Regents wore flat-topped square black hats embroidered with the Spellbinder sign. They stared sternly at Paul.

'You must kneel,' Ashka whispered.

Paul quickly knelt on the cold stone floor.

The door suddenly burst open and Correon, an old grey-haired Regent, stormed in, putting on his Regent's hat. 'It's impossible to work in this place,' he complained loudly. 'What horrendous crime has dragged me from my studies today? Has somebody stolen the eye of a needle?'

'This boy is accused of using magic,' Lukan said. 'He also stole an Eyestone.'

Correon looked at Paul, then suddenly yelled 'Boo' in his ear. Paul jumped. Correon chuckled and took the vacant seat at the table. 'If he's a magician, then I'm a frog. Banish him to the Wastelands and let me get back to my books.'

'Do something!' Paul whispered to Ashka.

'Silence!' Lukan ordered.

'Regents, don't be too hasty,' Ashka began. 'I believe the boy is not what he seems.'

Marna beckoned to Paul. 'Come here, boy.'

Paul got up and went to her. Marna took his hand and gave him a kindly smile. As he smiled back, Marna pricked Paul's finger with a needle. Paul yelped. Marna looked at the drop of blood that oozed out. 'He has red blood,' she announced. 'At least we know he's human.'

'And he broke the law,' said Correon. 'He must be punished!'

'The boy may have useful knowledge,' Ashka argued. 'The Summoner of Clayhill reported that he drove off a Marauder raiding party.'

'You shouldn't believe the reports of superstitious villagers,' Lukan chided.

Marna nodded. 'They still believe that the mountains hold up the sky.'

The Regents laughed.

'With respect, Regents, you should be more concerned,' Ashka said. 'The Marauder attacks are increasing.'

'Well, they can't be much of a threat if a boy

can drive them away,' Correon told her. 'I say banish him.'

'But I'm from another world!' Paul protested.

The Regents stared at him.

'I didn't use magic,' Paul explained desperately. 'It was science. And I didn't know it was wrong to take the Eyestone!'

'But you admit you took it?' Lukan asked.

'Yes. But ...'

'A confession,' Correon cried.

'Guilty by his own admission,' Marna declared.

'The sentence is banishment,' Lukan decided. 'Take him away.'

In desperation, Paul pulled the air-horn from his pants and pushed the button. Ashka and the Regents clapped their hands over their ears as the deafening screech reverberated around the chamber.

'Look,' Paul cried, holding it up. 'There's nothing like this in your world.' He handed the air-horn to Lukan.

Lukan turned it over in his hands, wondering how such a small object could make such a big noise. He pressed the button and the horn blasted him in the face. He dropped it and Correon picked it up.

'Where did you find this?' Correon asked Paul.

'I didn't find it. I brought it from my world. There's some other stuff in Ashka's room.'

The Regents looked at Ashka, who glared at Paul.

'Take the boy to a cell,' Correon ordered. 'We will decide what to with him after I have examined his things. Bring them to my rooms.'

Ashka bowed and pulled Paul towards the door. 'I told you not to say anything,' she snarled as she led him away from the Regents' chamber.

'I thought you were going to help me.'

'I am. But I can't go against the orders of the Regents.' Ashka led Paul through the castle to a barred door where two guards were standing. 'Don't despair,' she said kindly, 'I will help you. Trust me.'

One of the guards pushed Paul through the door. Paul looked in dismay at the bare interior of the prison cell. The guard went to a bunk and nudged a body under the blanket. 'You've got company.'

A figure crept out from behind the cell door. Paul recognised Zander, the youth with the flying toy at the market. The guard pulled back the blanket, revealing a stool and a pillow. Zander ran out of the cell.

'Escape!' the guard yelled.

From outside came the sound of a scuffle. The other guard hauled Zander back in and threw him on the floor. The guards left, slamming and bolting the door. Zander sat up, rubbing his head.

'I met you in Rivertown, remember?' Paul said. 'I helped you with your flying toy.'

Zander nodded glumly. 'How could I forget?'

'Why are you here?'

'The Spellbinders wanted to know what I was doing with a Marauder.'

'I'm not a Marauder,' Paul protested.

'It doesn't matter,' Zander replied. 'The Regents found me guilty anyway because of my toys. They said that only birds and

Spellbinders were meant to fly. They're taking me to the Wastelands today.'

'What are these Wastelands?' Paul asked.

'The land beyond the mountains. Nothing lives there. No trees. No animals. Even the water is poisoned. The Spellbinders take you there in a flying ship and leave you.'

'Then what happens?'

'What do you think?'

Paul went cold inside as he realised what Zander meant.

'Hey, Alex,' Smithy yelled as Alex walked into the schoolyard. 'Have the cops found Paul yet?'

'They're still looking,' Alex told his friend.

Smithy's mate, Giannos, came over, grinning lewdly. 'What were you and Paul doing up at the cave with those girls anyway?' he asked.

Smithy winked at him. 'What do you think?'

'I know what happened,' Giannos said

mysteriously. 'You went up to the cave that night and found Paul going the big pash with Katrina. So you got insanely jealous and bumped Paul off.'

'Rack off!' Alex yelled.

'Then you and Katrina buried the body,' Giannos continued. 'How can you live with your guilty secret?'

'Here comes your girlfriend now,' Smithy leered.

Alex groaned as he saw Katrina approaching, carrying a book.

'I know I'm going to sound crazy,' she said excitedly to Alex, 'but I think Paul's in another dimension. You know how ships and planes and things disappear in the Bermuda Triangle? The same thing must have happened to Paul.'

'You're right,' Alex said. 'You do sound crazy.'

Alex went into the boys' toilet. Smithy and Giannos gaped as Katrina followed him in. Two embarrassed boys raced out.

Katrina walked along the line of stalls and knocked on the only closed door. 'Alex?'

'Katrina, get out!' Alex yelled. 'This is really embarrassing.'

'Alex, you've got to listen. Have you heard of the many worlds theory?'

'Are they a band?' Alex asked, wishing that Katrina would go away.

'No! It's from quantum physics.' Katrina slid her book under the door. 'There's a theory that an infinite number of worlds exist at the same time, parallel to ours. I think that's where Paul is. In a parallel world.'

Alex came out of the stall holding the book. 'You are crazy!'

'What other explanation is there?'

'How about he's been abducted by aliens?'

Before Katrina could reply, Ms Gibson came in. 'Katrina, if you want to talk to Alex, please do it somewhere else. There's a queue of boys outside with bursting bladders.'

A crowd of boys greeted Alex and Katrina with jeers and catcalls as they emerged. Alex flushed with embarrassment.

'Come over to my place after school,' Katrina whispered to him. 'I've got a whole lot more stuff to show you.'

'No way!' Alex started to go but Katrina grabbed his hand.

'If you don't, I'll tell everyone what you and I were doing in the toilet.'

'We weren't doing anything!' Alex protested.

'We know that. But nobody else does.'

Alex looked at the boys watching them. Giannos and Smithy were sniggering. 'All right,' he said and stormed away.

Katrina smiled to herself.

Paul sat on the bunk watching Zander anxiously pacing the cell.

'Ashka's promised to look after me,' Paul said. 'Maybe I can get her to help you too.'

'Do you think she would?' Zander asked hopefully.

The door opened and the two guards entered. 'You,' one said, pointing at Zander. 'Come with us.'

Paul stepped in front of the guards. 'Hang on a minute. Go and get Ashka.'

One guard pushed Paul onto the bunk. The other grabbed Zander and pulled him towards the door.

Paul leaped up. 'Wait!'

One of the guards pulled out his club and Paul raised his hands to defend himself.

'No, Paul,' Zander cried. 'There's nothing you can do.'

Paul dropped his arms and watched in despair as the guards led Zander out of the cell. The door clanged shut. Paul huddled on the bunk, trembling with fear.

Deep in the forest, Riana sat listening to Paul's Walkman as pigeon meat cooked on a stick over a fire. She was lost and had decided to eat while she made up her mind what to do.

A flock of birds suddenly rose into the air. Riana saw them and pulled off the headphones. She heard a horse approaching and rolled into the undergrowth just as it appeared. Riana was surprised to see that the rider was Gryvon.

Gryvon saw the cooking meat and trotted over to the fire. 'Hello?' he called. Hearing no reply, he leaned down and grabbed the meat.

Hidden behind a bush, Riana growled softly.

'The Spellbinders thank you for dinner,' Gryvon called as he rode away, eating Riana's pigeon.

Riana crawled out of the undergrowth and stood up. Gryvon had stolen her dinner. In return, he could show her the way to the castle. Riana kicked out the fire and trotted after him.

Alex reluctantly followed Katrina into her bedroom. Her desk and floor were covered with books and articles about quantum physics and weird happenings. Katrina picked up a book entitled *Stranger than Fiction*. 'This is about unexplained disappearances. You'd be amazed at how many there are. Take a look. I've marked the relevant pages.' She held out the book but Alex didn't take it. 'It won't take long,' she added briskly.

'Look,' Alex confessed, 'I don't read real well, OK?'

'Why didn't you say so?'

'I just did!'

Katrina opened the book to a marked page. 'This is the best one. In Scotland, 200 years ago, a woman was struck by lightning and disappeared. Lots of people saw it. A year later, she was found in Paris.'

'So what are you saying? Paul's in Paris?'

'Don't be an idiot! This woman had no idea how she got to Paris but she talked about visiting a strange land.'

'Yeah, loonyland,' Alex scoffed. 'The goofiest kingdom of them all.'

'No,' Katrina said patiently. 'I think she'd been to a parallel world.' She slotted a tape into her video-recorder and pressed the play button. The screen showed a man standing in front of an electrical power station.

'There was this huge flash of energy,' the bewildered man was saying, 'and suddenly Bill wasn't there any more.' He held up a charred shoe. 'This is all I found of him. I think he got blasted into another dimension.'

Katrina pressed the pause button. 'A flash of energy,' she repeated, looking excitedly at

Alex. 'Just like what happened at the cave. See? It all adds up. Paul has to be in a parallel world. Unless we do something, he'll be stuck there forever.'

Alex stared at the man on the screen, not knowing what to think.

There were still wisps of morning mist in the air as Riana trotted along the forest trail, trying to stamp some warmth into her feet. Once it had become too dark to follow the prints of Gryvon's horse, Riana had climbed into a tree to sleep and now she was stiff, cold and hungry. Then she stopped and sniffed. She smelt smoke and cooking food. The smell made her mouth water. A horse snorted nearby. Riana crept forward and peered around a tree.

Stripped to the waist, Gryvon was washing in a stream, sluicing water over his head and shoulders. Behind him, several metres up the bank, a pot sat steaming over a fire. Using Gryvon's horse as cover, Riana darted to the pot and hungrily scooped stew into her mouth with a spoon.

She was about to go when she noticed some horse dung on the ground and smiled wickedly. She grabbed a handful and dropped it into the pot, quickly mixing it in with the remaining stew. Then she ran back to the tree.

Drying himself with his cloak, Gryvon returned to the fire. He stirred the pot then took a mouthful of stew. His face screwed up and he spat it out. 'You didn't?' he said to his horse in disgust.

Watching from her hiding place, Riana tried to stop herself laughing out loud.

Paul lay on the bunk trying to convince himself that this was all a dream and that when he opened his eyes, he would be back in his bed. He opened them and looked around: he was still in the cell. Then he heard a key turning in the lock. Paul sat up, hoping it would be Ashka.

'Stand up when I enter, prisoner,' Gryvon ordered.

134

Paul got slowly to his feet. 'You were wrong,

Gryvon,' he said defiantly. 'They didn't send me to the Wastelands.'

'... yet,' Gryvon answered ominously.

He showed Paul the fireworks he had found at Clayhill. 'Tell me how to release the magic in these and I'll make sure you're not banished.'

'What can you do?' Paul asked sceptically. 'You're just an Apprentice.'

'The Spellbinders are old, fixed in their ways. They'll never believe you're from some other world. I've seen your magic. Tell me how it works and I'll show them.'

'All right,' Paul agreed. 'But you must be careful. Gunpowder is dangerous.'

'Spellbinder, I've got something I think you'll find very interesting.'

Ashka looked up to see Gryvon hurrying through the castle gardens towards her. He bowed, then held out the two small clay pots.

'These are fireworks,' he said. 'They're what the boy used to defeat the Marauders. After careful study, I've been able to work out how to release their magic. Watch.' He pushed one of the fireworks into a pile of compost and lit the fuse. 'Stand back, Spellbinder,' he cautioned. 'The gunpowder is dangerous.'

Ashka didn't move. 'That little thing?' she snorted.

The firework exploded, covering Ashka with compost.

Terrified of the Spellbinder's wrath, Gryvon tried to brush the muck from her clothes. 'I'm sorry, Spellbinder. Forgive me.'

Ashka pushed him away. 'Go to the boy and get him to tell you how these fireworks are made. I must know the secret of this "gunpowder".'

'At once, Spellbinder.' Gryvon bowed and raced away.

Ashka picked up the second firework. She lit the fuse and dropped it into an urn. She placed a heavy stone over the top and moved back. The firework exploded with a loud bang and the urn shattered. Ashka smiled at the destructive result of her experiment.

Riana pushed her way wearily through the thick undergrowth. She was lost. Gryvon's trail had disappeared when he'd ridden down a stream. Riana laboured up a steep slope and stopped. A Spellbinder sign on a tree warned her to go no further. Then she became aware of a strange crackling sound.

Riana nervously skirted the sign and climbed to the top of the slope. Before her stood the forbidding Spellbinder castle. It was the biggest thing she had ever seen. It was so high that lightning crackled around the tower on the roof.

Riana froze. If she was found here, she would be banished. But if she went home, Paul would be sent to the Wastelands. For the first time in her life, Riana had no idea what she was supposed to do.

Show Me Your World

Hidden in the trees, Riana looked up at the grey stone walls of the enormous Spellbinder castle. A high circular tower rose above the roof, topped by a metal pylon. Dazzling bolts of electricity crackled around it. Grim-faced sentries in black leather uniforms stood guard outside massive metal-studded gates. Every fibre in Riana's body told her to turn round and go home. Then she remembered that Paul had saved her life and her brother's. She had to try and help him.

Further around the wall of the castle Riana could see a smaller gate where a lone sentry was inspecting an ox-cart piled with vegetables. She scrambled down the hillside and hurried up to the gate. 'Excuse me, sir,' she said respectfully, 'I have to see the Spellbinder Ashka.'

'Nobody goes into the castle but the Spellbinders and their Apprentices and servants,' the sentry said curtly. 'Now be on your way.'

'But I have to show her this.' Riana held out the videotape. The sentry took the odd-looking black box and examined it suspiciously. 'It belongs to the boy Ashka brought here,' Riana explained. 'It has pictures of another world.'

'Hey, Borin,' the sentry called, 'come and have a look at this.'

Another sentry came out of a guard hut. 'What is it now, Mort?' he grumbled.

'She says the box has pictures in it,' Mort replied.

Borin took the videotape and tried to open it.

'Be careful,' Riana cried. 'You could break it.'

'Get back to your village,' Mort snapped.

Borin tried to prise the videotape open with his knife. In desperation, Riana snatched it from him. Caught between the two sentries, Riana's only escape was to run inside the guard hut. She slammed the door and bolted it.

'Come out of there!' Borin yelled, pounding on the door. There was no reply. The two sentries charged the door. It crashed inwards and Mort and Borin sprawled into the hut. The back window was open but the hut was empty.

Riana lay on the roof as the sentries ran out and started looking for her. The ox-cart driver joined in the search. Knowing that they would soon find her, Riana dropped off the hut onto the cart and buried herself under the vegetables.

The sentries returned from their search, angry at having been outwitted by a girl. Mort went to the castle gate and rang a bell beside it.

'Looks like the Spellbinders will be eating well again,' he said, looking jealously at the plump vegetables on the cart. 'They get the best of everything.'

The cart driver took the hint and went to the back of his cart. Riana froze as he removed some turnips from in front of her face and gave them to Borin. A guard inside the castle opened the gate. Borin quickly stuffed the turnips under his tunic and waved the driver in. As the cart passed through the gate into a courtyard, Riana peered fearfully from under the vegetables. The gate clanged shut behind her.

Riana knew that she would be discovered as soon as the vegetables were unloaded. As the cart passed under a low wooden archway, she leaped up and grabbed a beam. She swung her legs up and clambered onto a balcony.

Huddled below a window, Riana wondered what to do next. A door at the end of the balcony opened and a youth wearing the uniform of an Apprentice walked out. Without thinking, Riana dived through the window.

Riana leaped to her feet, ready to run, but the room was empty. She looked around at the furnishings. Thick carpet covered the floor, and paintings and sculptures adorned the walls. Riana sat in a richly upholstered chair and was amazed at its softness. Then she remembered where she was and hurried to the door. She opened it a crack. The corridor outside was deserted. Riana crept out of the room, wondering how she was ever going to find Paul in this immense building.

Paul was luxuriating in a steaming bath in Ashka's apartment. Since Ashka had seen the fireworks explode, she had been very friendly to him. With her help, Paul felt sure he would get home. Now he could just lie back and enjoy the adventure. The door opened and Paul slid modestly under the water as Ashka came in.

'Feeling better?' she inquired.

'Much. The water's getting a bit cold, though.'

'Gryvon! More hot water.'

Gryvon came in, lugging a steaming bucket. He glared at Paul, slopped the hot water into the bath and stomped out. Ashka followed Gryvon out, closing the door behind her.

'I am an Apprentice, not a servant,' Gryvon complained. 'Why are you punishing me?'

'I'm not punishing you. I just want Paul to think I'm his friend.'

'Why?'

Ashka lifted a cloth on the table, revealing the shattered remains of the urn from the garden. 'One of his little fireworks did that. Imagine what a big one would do. I must have the secret of his gunpowder.'

'Why don't I just hold his head under the water until he tells us?' Gryvon suggested with a malicious grin.

Ashka shook her head. 'Who knows what other knowledge he may have? If Paul trusts me, he'll open up and talk. We can both gain a lot from him, Gryvon.'

Gryvon smiled. He went to the bathroom door and knocked. 'Paul,' he called politely, 'can I get you some more hot water?'

Alex came out of his house, ready for school, and was surprised to find Katrina waiting for him.

'I've had a great idea,' she announced. 'We'll show my research to Paul's father.' Katrina opened her bag. It was crammed with the books, photocopies and videotapes she had shown Alex the previous night.

Alex looked dubious. 'I don't know, Katrina. It sounds too weird.'

'Not to a scientist. Once Mr Reynolds sees this, he'll realise I'm right. Then he'll find a

143

way to rescue Paul from the parallel world.'

'So what do you need me for?'

'You're Paul's friend. His dad'll listen to you.'

Alex shook his head. 'Forget it.'

'If you don't help me,' Katrina threatened, 'I'll start telling everybody that I really am your girlfriend.'

Alex laughed. 'They'll never believe you.'

'They will when they see this.' Katrina took a sheet of paper from her bag. On it was drawn a big heart pierced by an arrow and the words 'A.K. LOVES K.M.' Under the heart was a typed letter. Katrina started to read: 'Dearest Katrina, goddess of my heart ...'

Alex snatched the paper and ripped it up.

'It's just a photocopy,' Katrina said, grinning. 'I've got plenty more. If you pike, Katsonis, by lunchtime tomorrow, everyone in the school is going to believe you've got the hots for me.'

Alex groaned.

'Deal?' Katrina asked.

Alex knew when he was beaten; he nodded.

Correon's apartment reverberated with the sound of Paul's air-horn. The old Regent sat at his desk, holding down the button on the can. Strips of cloth were stuffed in his ears to keep out the terrible noise. The wailing eventually faded and stopped. Correon shook the metal cylinder but no more sound would come out. He twisted the can but it wouldn't open. Correon picked his way through the clutter of ancient books on the floor and went to the fireplace. He clamped the can on a stand over the flames, hoping the heat would open it.

As he returned to his desk, Correon tripped over Paul's pack, which Ashka had sent to him. It lay half-buried under a pile of books. 'So that's where that is,' he murmured.

Correon pushed aside some books, put the pack on his desk and carefully took out the torch and video-camera. He picked up the camera and carried it through a side-door, studying it closely. As he went, the door to the corridor slowly opened and Riana peered in. She had followed the familiar sound of Paul's air-horn.

Riana looked around the chaotic apartment. 145

Every shelf, every table-top, even the floor, was covered with books, glass bottles and strange metal objects. There was no sign of Paul. Then Riana saw his pack on the table. 'Paul?' she whispered. There was no reply.

Riana stepped into the room just as Correon reappeared with the camera. She dived under the desk. The old Spellbinder sat in his chair, his feet centimetres from Riana's face. The girl dared not move.

In the fireplace, the air-horn glowed red-hot. Suddenly it exploded, hurling Correon to the floor. He found himself staring at Riana.

'Who are you?' he yelled. 'How did you get inside the castle?'

Trembling with fear, Riana scrambled to her feet and bowed. 'I'm sorry, Spellbinder.'

'Speak up,' Correon shouted. 'I can't hear you.'

Riana pulled the cloth from Correon's ears. 'My name is Riana, Spellbinder,' she said. 'I came to help Paul.'

'The boy who claims he is from another world?'

'He is. I can prove it. That's his camera.'

Riana pointed to the camera, and then held up the videotape. 'I brought the picture box that makes it work. I can show you Paul's world.'

'Show me,' Correon said.

Riana picked up the camera and tried to remember what Paul had done. She found the place where the videotape went and pushed it in. There was a whirring sound. Riana turned the camera around and started pushing buttons. A red light flashed on the camera but nothing else happened.

'Don't point it at me,' Correon snapped. 'It may be dangerous.'

'It's not. It just collects pictures. Moving pictures.'

'Give it to me,' Correon demanded.

'Wait,' Riana said, backing away, 'I know I can do it.' She pressed more buttons.

'Do you dare to deny a Spellbinder?' Correon roared.

Suddenly his face appeared on the screen on the back of the camera. 'Don't point that at me. It may be dangerous,' came Correon's voice from the tiny loudspeaker.

Correon grabbed the camera and stared at

himself on the screen. 'How did I get in there?'

Paul sat at the table in Ashka's apartment, stuffed to bursting from the huge meal he had just consumed. Ashka and Gryvon sat at the other end of the table.

'I can't wait to get home and tell my dad about all this,' Paul said.

Ashka smiled. 'I'm sure we can persuade the Regents to help you get home ... if you do something for them in return.'

'Like what?' Paul asked.

Ashka got up and went to a map hanging on the wall. 'This is the Spellbinders' land.'

She pointed to a green region surrounded by mountains. A miniature drawing of the Spellbinder's castle was in the centre. A network of Summoning Towers was drawn around it. There was a village near each tower.

'What's out here?' Paul asked, pointing to the dark region beyond the mountains.

'The Wastelands,' Ashka said. 'Where the Marauders come from. When the Darkness came, everything but our land was destroyed.'

Paul was shocked. 'The rest of the world is dead?'

Gryvon nodded grimly. 'Only the power of the Spellbinders saved us.'

'What caused this Darkness?' Paul asked.

'The Marauders,' Gryvon replied angrily.

'And now they are back, destroying our villages and stealing our crops,' Ashka said. 'If you show us how to make your gunpowder, all these villages could be protected.'

'That's easy,' Paul told her. 'You just need ...'

Before he could say more, the door burst open and Correon stormed in. 'What is the boy doing here?' he demanded. 'The Regents ordered that he be kept in a cell.'

'I know, Regent Correon,' Ashka replied hurriedly. 'But he was badly in need of a bath.'

'Do you offer baths to all our prisoners?' Correon sneered. 'Come with me, boy.' He pulled Paul towards the door. Paul grabbed a piece of cake from the table and hid it under his clothes as Correon dragged him out. The door slammed shut after them.

With a cry of rage, Ashka hurled her glass at

the door. 'Follow him, Gryvon. Find out what he's up to.'

Gryvon was horrified. 'You want me to spy on a Regent?'

'Do you want to be an Apprentice all your life?' Ashka roared. 'Go!'

Gryvon went.

'Are you taking me back to the cell?' Paul asked anxiously as he followed Correon through the castle gardens.

'No. To my rooms. I want you to explain how my likeness got into this.' Correon held out the videotape.

'My tape,' Paul exclaimed. 'Where did you get it?'

Correon said nothing and kept walking. Unseen, Gryvon crept after them.

'Riana,' Paul cried with delight as he followed Correon through the door. 'You brought the tape. Thank you!' He hugged Riana. But then a look of dismay appeared on his face and he pushed her away.

'What's wrong?' Riana asked.

Paul took the squashed remains of the cake from under his shirt. 'I thought Correon was taking me back to the cell,' he explained. 'I didn't know when I'd get to eat again.'

'Show me the moving pictures,' Correon ordered, holding out the camera.

'The Regents will have to believe I'm from another world when they see this,' Paul crowed. He put the tape in the camera and pressed the rewind button.

Outside in the corridor, Gryvon peered through the keyhole. The last person he'd expected to see was Riana.

Riana was looking at one of Correon's strange metal objects. It was a set of concentric metal rings mounted on a spindle. On each ring was a brass ball. She touched one of the balls and the rings began to rotate around a central brass sphere.

'Leave that alone,' Correon snapped.

'What is it?' Riana asked.

'It's just a toy.'

Paul looked at the device and realised it was an orrery. 'It's a model of the solar system,' he said in amazement. 'Look, Riana. The world is round. And it goes around the sun.'

Correon pushed Paul over to the camera.
'Show me your world.'

Paul pressed the play button. The screen
showed the grimy industrial landscape that
Alex had taped through the school bus
window.

'What are they?' Correon asked, pointing at
the chimneys belching smoke.

'Factories,' Paul replied. 'Buildings where we
make things.'

Correon shook his head in disbelief. 'You're
right, Paul,' he said. 'The Regents will believe
you. There is nothing like that horror in this
world.'

Katrina's research was spread across a coffee
table in Paul's loungeroom. Alex listened
anxiously as Katrina expounded her theory to
Paul's father.

'And here,' she said, opening another book,
'a farmer reported that his prize cow was hit by
lightning and disappeared.'

'This is nonsense,' Brian said. 'There's no scientific basis to any of it.'

Katrina pointed to a map. 'But there's magnetic rock all around the cave where Paul disappeared.'

'So?' Brian asked.

'So the magnetic rocks and the power surge down the cable created an electromagnetic doorway, and Paul was sucked into a parallel world.'

'You've got no idea what you're talking about,' Brian said impatiently.

'But I saw Paul,' Katrina cried.

'Where is he?' a small voice asked.

They all turned to see Christine, Paul's sister, standing in the doorway.

Brian went to her. 'Don't get excited, sweetheart,' he said gently. 'I'm afraid Katrina's made a mistake. Now go upstairs; I'll be up in a second.'

Christine did as she was told.

'I think you'd better leave,' Brian told Alex and Katrina.

'But we've got to get some sort of electro-magnetic generator up to the cave,' Katrina protested. 'If we can recreate the effect, we might be able to get Paul back.'

'Katrina, I know you're trying to help but there's a much simpler explanation,' Brian said patiently. 'A boy answering Paul's description was seen in the bush near Gidgewarrup. That's only thirty kilometres from the cave. The police are searching there now and I'm going to join them.'

'That's great,' Alex said, hoping it was Paul.

Katrina angrily threw the research into her bag and headed for the door.

'Sorry for bothering you, Mr Reynolds,' Alex called as he followed her out.

Alex caught up to Katrina as she strode away from the house. 'Maybe the kid in the bush is Paul.'

'He can't be! Paul's in a parallel world.' Katrina angrily threw her bag down. It fell open and papers blew along the street. Alex started picking them up. 'What's the point?' Katrina said despondently. 'No-one will believe me.'

'I do,' Alex said quietly.

'You're just saying that. You didn't see

anything at the cave.'

'Well, actually, I ... er ...'

'You did see something!'

'Before the cable came down I think I might have,' Alex admitted. 'It could have been Paul.'

'Why didn't you say so?'

'I don't know what I saw. I didn't want everyone to think I was crazy. So what do we do now?'

'We have to get back up to the cave and try and find a way into the other world. We're the only ones who know the truth, Alex. We're the only hope Paul's got.'

Gryvon was hiding on a staircase in the Regents' chamber. Below him, Correon turned the video-camera off. Astounded by what they had just seen, Lukan and Marna stared at Paul.

'Do you have power suits in your world?' Marna asked.

'No,' Paul answered.

The Regents looked relieved.

'But we have lasers and missiles and   155

computers,' Paul said. 'They're machines that think a billion times faster than a person. Compared to us, you guys are back in the Stone Age.'

'We have flying ships,' Marna reminded him.

'And we have rockets that have flown men to the moon,' Paul boasted.

'That's impossible,' Lukan declared. 'The moon is too small to stand on. It's only as big as an apple.'

Paul laughed. 'Don't give me that. Correon's got a model of the solar system in his room. You guys know all about the moon and the planets.'

Lukan glared at Correon. 'Why did you let him see it?'

'Everyone in my world knows that stuff from primary school,' Paul told the Regents. 'Why are you keeping it secret?'

'The Spellbinders decide what the people should know,' Marna said sharply. 'It's for their own good.'

'It's for your good,' Paul said. 'You have all the knowledge and power, and everyone else gets treated like slaves.'

'I've heard enough,' Lukan roared. 'No matter where the boy comes from, he has broken the law.'

'But his knowledge could be valuable,' Marna argued. 'Perhaps he can help us repair our flying ships?'

'No,' Lukan snapped, 'he already knows too much about us. Banish him!'

'I think we should question him further,' Correon said.

Marna nodded. Lukan was outvoted.

'Very well,' he said grudgingly. 'Take him back to his cell.'

Correon picked up the camera and led Paul out of the chamber.

'They're not going to let me go, are they?' Paul asked as they went back to the cells.

'You should not have argued with Lukan,' Correon said. 'Tomorrow, you must apologise to him.'

They passed a window. In the courtyard outside, a flying ship was landing in a shower of sparks.

'What did Marna mean about repairing the flying ships?' Paul asked.

'They were built before the Darkness, when the Spellbinders had great knowledge,' Correon told him. 'Now we don't even understand how they fly. If one breaks we can't repair it. We only have six left that work. We have the same problem with our power suits. All my studies are an attempt to regain our lost knowledge. Perhaps you can help.'

Correon came into his apartment and found Riana asleep on a bed of books. He nudged her with his foot. 'Get up. Those are for reading, not for sleeping on.'

Riana scrambled to her feet and bowed to Correon.

'Spellbinder, did the Regents believe Paul's story?'

'They were very impressed,' Correon said, to Riana's relief.

'When can I go home?' she asked.

'I'm sorry, Riana. You have seen too much of the Spellbinders' world. You can never leave the castle. You must stay here as a servant.'

Riana was horrified. 'But I want to go back to my village.'

'It is a great honour to serve the Spell-binders,' Correon said.

'I don't want to be a servant,' Riana cried. 'I want to be home with my family.'

'The alternative is banishment,' Correon said bluntly. 'Someone will come to fetch you.'

Correon went out and closed the door. Riana heard it lock. Desperately she looked around but there was no other way out.

Paul sat up as the door to his cell opened. He was surprised to see Ashka and Gryvon.

'Get up, Paul,' Ashka said urgently. 'You must go with Gryvon. The Regents have decided to banish you.'

'But Correon said ...'

'Correon is an old fool,' Gryvon snarled.

Paul looked uncertain.

'I promised to help you get home,' Ashka said. 'Do you want to go or not?'

Paul didn't need asking twice; he followed Gryvon out.

As soon as they had gone, Ashka hid behind the open door. 'Help! Guard!' she called.

There was the sound of footsteps hurrying

towards the cell. As the guard came through the doorway, Ashka slammed the door in his face. With a thud he collapsed to the floor. Ashka opened the door and quickly dragged him inside.

'Where are you taking me?' Paul asked as Gryvon hurried him through the castle gardens.

'Somewhere the Regents won't find you.'

Gryvon led Paul down a flight of steps leading to a heavy wooden door at the base of the castle wall. Gryvon unbolted the door and threw it open. 'Welcome to your new home.'

Paul stepped through the doorway. Cobwebs hung thickly from the ceiling and walls of the musty cellar. Old furniture covered in dust was strewn around the damp floor.

'How long will I have to stay here?' Paul asked uneasily.

Gryvon smiled. 'How long will it take you to make the gunpowder?'

A key turned in the lock of Correon's door. Riana stood beside the door on a chair, a large book raised above her head. She wasn't going to become a servant without putting up a fight.

The door opened and Ashka entered. Riana brought the book down but Ashka saw the movement and sidestepped. The book missed. Riana leaped from the chair and tried to run out of the door but Ashka grabbed her. Riana struggled furiously.

'Stop it, girl. I've come to help you,' Ashka said. 'I've been trying to get Paul out of the castle but he won't go without you. But if you want to stay here as a servant for the rest of your days ...' Ashka let Riana go and turned to leave.

'Wait!' Riana cried.

Riana followed Ashka through the castle to the cells. Ashka unlocked a barred door and beckoned for Riana to enter. Inside the cell, Riana saw a figure lying on the bunk under a blanket.

'Paul!', she cried, pulling back the blanket.

The guard whom Ashka had knocked out, was underneath. Riana turned to Ashka, a chill of fear passing through her.

'Guard! Guard!' Ashka yelled out of the door.

A guard ran into the cell and stared at his unconscious comrade.

'She helped the boy escape,' Ashka said, pointing at Riana. 'Grab her!'

Riana realised she had been tricked. She backed away from the guard and felt the cell wall behind her back. She was trapped.

The Gunpowder Plot

As the guard moved towards her, Riana pulled the blanket from the bunk and threw it over his head. She pushed the surprised guard into Ashka and they fell to the floor. Riana leaped over them and raced out of the cell.

'Stop her!' Ashka screamed.

Riana fled down a staircase and raced along a deserted corridor. She ran through a door at the end and found herself in the castle gardens. Hearing sounds of pursuit, Riana leaped a flower bed and ran up a flight of stone steps leading to a balcony. Below her, Ashka and the guard burst into the gardens. Riana dropped out of sight behind a railing where some servants' uniforms were hanging out to dry. As Ashka and the guard began to search for her, Riana grabbed one of the uniforms and crept away.

Paul looked unhappily around the dingy cellar. A rat scurried across the floor. He wondered if he should have stayed in the cell.

'I'm sorry that I treated you badly,' Gryvon said as he lit a torch. 'But you must admit that your story was difficult to believe.'

'I still have trouble believing it myself,' Paul admitted.

'Can we start again?' Gryvon asked. 'I'd like to be your friend.' He gave Paul a big smile.

Paul thought it had all the warmth of an iceberg. 'Just help me to get back to my own world,' he said.

'As soon as you show us how to make fireworks, you'll be on your way.'

Paul looked suspiciously at Gryvon. 'How do I know Ashka will keep her promise?'

Gryvon put his arm around Paul's shoulders. 'Trust us, Paul. We'll help you get home. We got you out of the cell, didn't we? Now, please, what do you need to make the gunpowder?'

'Charcoal, sulphur—which you call goodyellow ...' Paul began. He stopped when he saw that Gryvon was writing everything down. He realised that if Ashka had the formula for gunpowder, she would have no reason to help him. '... and hot peppers,' Paul continued. He smiled to himself as Gryvon added it to the list.

Riana crept warily through the castle, wearing the servant's uniform and carrying a feather duster she had found. Ashka came storming up the corridor. Riana turned away and began dusting a statue. Ashka passed her without a glance, and opened the door to her apartment.

'Ashka!' Correon shouted from the end of the corridor.

Riana kept her face averted as the old Spellbinder approached. Ashka left the open doorway and went towards him.

'Has the girl been found?' Correon asked.

'Not yet,' Ashka replied. 'I'm afraid she might have escaped the castle with the boy. I've got guards searching the forest.'

Anger flashed in Correon's eyes. 'Order them to search the castle as well. I want the boy found. And I want her sent straight to the Wastelands.'

As Correon strode away, Ashka yelled for the castle guards. Riana tried to sneak away but guards appeared in the corridor ahead. Fearing she would be caught, Riana slipped through Ashka's open door. She looked around for somewhere to hide, and dived under the bed just before Ashka came in.

'I want every room searched,' Ashka told the guards. 'When you find the girl, bring her straight to me.'

'Shall we search your room first?' a guard asked.

'If she was in here, I wouldn't be asking you to search, would I?' Ashka slammed the door in the guard's face. Beneath the bed, Riana breathed a sigh of relief.

There was a knock on the door and Gryvon came in holding a sheet of paper. 'I've got the list of ingredients for gunpowder,' he said proudly to Ashka.

'Good. Make sure you list everything he does. Once we learn his secret, we can be rid of him.'

Gryvon bowed and went out. Ashka took off her boots and lay down on the bed, closing her eyes.

Trapped beneath the bed, Riana realised that she must find Paul quickly. But she dared not move for fear of disturbing the Spellbinder. She had no choice but to wait.

Alex felt terrible as he entered the bustling schoolyard. He'd lain awake most of the night thinking about Paul. How were he and Katrina going to rescue him from a place that might not even exist?

'Alex!'

Alex saw Katrina running towards him.

'How much money have you got?' she asked excitedly.

Alex reached into his pocket and pulled out some coins. 'About a dollar twenty.'

'We're going to need a lot more than that.'

'Why?'

Katrina grinned. 'I've found a way of getting us up to the cave. Two kids from Year 10 are going on a study camp to Mount Lara this weekend. We can bribe them to let us take their places.'

'I've got about a hundred bucks,' Alex said reluctantly, 'but I'm saving it for new fishing gear.'

'Alex! We're trying to save Paul's life.'

'All right. I'll go to the bank at lunchtime.'

Katrina gave Alex a hug. He squirmed away, embarrassed. 'So what kind of camp is this?' he asked.

'A literature camp.'

'Literature? Katrina! I've never even finished a book.'

Katrina smiled. 'Now's your chance.'

Paul was heating an iron pot over a fire when the cellar door opened, and Gryvon came in carrying a wooden box.

'Did you get everything?' Paul asked.

'Yes,' Gryvon said grumpily. 'It took me most of the night.' He put the box down and took out two dried cowpats.

'What is the purpose of the cow dung?'

'It's a catalyst,' Paul said, trying to keep a straight face. 'That's a scientific term.'

Gryvon wrote this information on his sheet of paper.

'You'll need to grind it finely,' Paul said. 'But let's start with the bacon.'

Gryvon pulled a slab of bacon from the box.

'Cut me three slices,' Paul instructed. 'Not too thin.'

Gryvon did so and gave them to Paul. 'Do you mix the bacon with the cow dung?' he asked.

'No! The bacon isn't for the gunpowder. It's for breakfast.' Paul dropped the bacon into the hot pot and smiled at Gryvon. 'Did you bring the eggs?'

'You didn't even touch the bath last time,' Ashka roared.

Riana awoke with a start and peered out from under the bed. Two frightened servants stood by the door as Ashka bellowed at them. 'I want it spotless. And don't forget to sweep all the floors.'

Ashka strode out. The servants scurried into the bathroom and got to work. Seeing her chance, Riana slid out from under the bed. She grabbed a broom one of the servants had left behind and sneaked out into the corridor.

Paul ladled some soot into the iron pot, then dropped in three of the hot peppers. Gryvon held out a stone mortar which contained a finely ground white powder. 'I have finished grinding the bittercrystal.'

'Good. Put a pinch in here.'

Gryvon carefully dropped a pinch of saltpetre into the tall jar Paul was holding.

'Now add half a cup of baking soda. Then a cup of vinegar.'

Gryvon followed Paul's instructions and the mixture started to froth.

'Seal the jar and shake it,' Paul said quickly.

Gryvon jammed a cork in the jar and shook it vigorously. The gas generated by the chemical reaction blew the cork out of the jar and covered Gryvon in thick white foam.

'Perfect,' Paul said, trying not to laugh. 'Now take it to the top of the castle and expose it to sunlight for an hour. You have to keep stirring it or it will burst into flames.'

Gryvon wrote the instructions down and hurried out, bolting the cellar door behind him. Paul laughed at Gryvon's gullibility. He picked up the mortar containing the saltpetre and started making the real gunpowder.

'Did you get it?' Katrina asked eagerly as Alex sauntered up to the school gate where she was waiting.

'I emptied the account: 120 bucks.' Alex produced some bank notes and handed them over.

Katrina pointed to a tall, tough-looking girl and a short bespectacled boy approaching them from across the yard. 'That's them,' Katrina said.

Alex groaned. 'Not Deanna McDougall!'

'Do you know her?'

'We went to primary school together. She hates me.'

'Just be nice to her. Hi, Nathan. Hi, Deanna,' Katrina said as the couple arrived.

'You're looking great, Deanna,' Alex gushed.

'You used to be such a squirt. You've really changed.'

'Pity you haven't, Katsonis,' Deanna retorted. 'You're still a creep.'

Alex smiled through gritted teeth.

'Why are you two so keen to go on this camp?' Nathan inquired.

'Well, we both love literature,' Katrina began.

'Get real,' Deanna interrupted, 'Alex had to repeat third grade because he didn't know the alphabet. He's never read a book in his life.'

'Who cares about books?' Alex declared, thinking quickly. 'The bottom line is, Katrina and I love each other but her parents won't let me see her.'

Katrina gaped at Alex.

'Star-crossed lovers,' Nathan sighed. 'Like Romeo and Juliet. How romantic.'

'Going on this camp is the only chance we have to be together.' Alex took Katrina's hand. 'Isn't it, darling?'

Deanna sneered. 'Katrina, you can't seriously like this illiterate furball.'

'Um, he's really nice when you get to know him.' Katrina smiled dreamily at Alex, then looked at Deanna and Nathan. 'So, do we have a deal?'

'How much is it worth to you?' Deanna asked.

'Fifty dollars?'

Nathan's eyes went wide. 'Wow!'

'Each,' Deanna said.

'Now hang on,' Alex protested.

'I thought you were in love with each other,' Deanna reminded him.

Alex watched in dismay as Katrina handed over his two fifty-dollar notes and gave them each a sheet of paper. 'Show these notes to your parents,' she said. 'They explain that the camp's been cancelled.'

Deanna walked away, pocketing the note and the money.

'I want to hear all about your romantic weekend when you get back,' Nathan said. 'I might make it the basis for my first novel.' He went after Deanna.

Alex batted his eyes at Katrina. 'Well, that went pretty well, darling.'

'Don't push your luck,' Katrina snapped. 'Meet me after school and we'll figure out how to get our parents to let us go.' She started to leave.

'What about my change?' Alex asked.

Katrina handed him the remaining twenty-dollar note.

'Twenty bucks?' Alex exclaimed. 'Didn't you put any of your money in?'

'I'm broke.'

Alex grimaced. 'This had better be worth it.'

Paul was grinding the black grains of gunpowder in the mortar when the bolt on the cellar door was drawn. He quickly hid the mortar under the table and pulled over the pot containing the fake gunpowder.

Gryvon came in, carefully carrying the tall jar. 'I didn't stop stirring it,' he announced. 'It didn't catch fire.'

'Well done. Pour it in here. Carefully.' Gryvon poured the small amount of remaining liquid into the pot. Paul gave it a quick stir. 'There. The gunpowder is finished. Now we need small clay pots to make the fireworks.' Gryvon hurried out.

Paul took the pot with the fake gunpowder to a dark corner and tipped it out. Then he poured the real gunpowder into the empty pot. Everything was going according to plan.

Still dressed in the servant's uniform, Riana was wearily sweeping a corridor. She had swept more than twenty rooms without finding any sign of Paul. She saw Ashka and Gryvon approaching and hid behind a pillar. Gryvon was carrying a box filled with small clay pots.

'Paul and I should finish making the fireworks before sunset,' Gryvon said.

'Good. We'll test them tonight.'

They continued along the corridor. Riana followed them through the castle and out into garden where she watched them descend the steps.

Paul looked up as Ashka and Gryvon entered the cellar.

'Show me the gunpowder,' Ashka commanded.

Paul pointed to the iron pot. Ashka picked up a candle to see better.

'No!' Paul yelled and pushed her away.

Behind them the cellar door opened a crack and Riana peered through.

Ashka turned angrily on Paul. 'You dare to touch me?'

'I'm sorry, Spellbinder, but the flame would have exploded the gunpowder. See?' Paul dropped a pinch of gunpowder into the candle flame. It ignited with a whoosh and a puff of smoke.

Ashka smiled. 'I want to test the fireworks tonight.'

'We can't do it here,' Paul protested. 'We'll wake up the whole castle.'

'Very well. We'll go to the ruins at dawn. No-one will hear us there.' As Ashka turned towards the door, Riana ducked back out of sight.

'Then you'll help me get home?' Paul asked hopefully.

'If the test is successful.' Gryvon followed Ashka out, closing the door.

Riana crouched at the top of the stairs outside the cellar and listened as Ashka whispered to Gryvon: 'Have you got a record of everything the boy has done?'

'Of course.'

'Then make some gunpowder of your own. If yours works as well as the boy's, we will have no further use for him.'

Gryvon nodded and went back into the cellar. Ashka started to climb the stairs. Riana huddled out of sight as she passed. She waited a moment, then crept back down the stairs to the cellar door. As she reached for the door handle, a hand seized her shoulder. It was Ashka. Riana tried to yell a warning to Paul but Ashka clamped a hand over her mouth.

'Gryvon!' Ashka called.

Gryvon came out of the cellar and saw Riana. He quickly bolted the door and helped Ashka drag the struggling girl up the stairs.

Ashka and Gryvon carried Riana into Ashka's bathroom. Her hands and feet were tied with rope.

'No-one will find her here,' Ashka said as they lowered Riana into the bath.

'What are you going to do with her?'
Gryvon asked.

'I don't know,' Ashka replied. 'But if Paul
causes any trouble, we'll let him know we've
got her. Wake me at dawn.'

As soon as they left, Riana began struggling
with the cords binding her wrists. The knots
wouldn't give.

Riana put her wrists in the water in the
bottom of the bath and soaked the cords. She
lifted the softened cords to her mouth and
started to chew.

Katrina was watching television with her
mother. Although it was Katrina's favourite
program, she kept casting impatient glances at
the phone. As soon as it rang, she leaped up
and grabbed it. 'Hello? ... Oh hi, sir. Mum, it's
Mr Vass from school. He wants to talk to you.'

'What about?'

'I don't know.'

Katrina handed the phone to her mother.

Alex and his older brother, Nick, were in

their garage. Nick had the phone and was reading from a piece of paper that Alex held.

'Sorry to disturb you, Mrs Muggleton,' Nick read. 'Two of our students were going on a literature camp this weekend but one of them's sick. I was wondering if Katrina would like to take her place.'

Nick held out his hand and Alex reluctantly put the twenty-dollar note in it.

'Wonderful,' Nick continued. 'She'll be picked up outside the school at 8.30 tomorrow morning.' Alex thrust another piece of paper at Nick. 'There's a 120 dollar fee,' Nick added. 'Cash would be preferable ... Thank you. Good night.' Nick hung up. The brothers grinned at each other.

The sky outside the bathroom window was just beginning to lighten as Riana sat in the bath, still doggedly chewing the ropes. Her jaw ached but she had nearly bitten through one of the cords around her wrists. Gryvon came in and Riana quickly hid her hands.

'Gryvon,' she pleaded, 'we're from the same village. Help me.'

Gryvon looked at her contemptuously. 'You never should have left Clayhill, Riana.'

'Did you bring your gunpowder?' Ashka asked from the doorway.

Gryvon held up a sack. 'I followed Paul's instructions exactly.'

'Good. Let's go.'

As they went out, Riana desperately resumed chewing.

Gryvon crept into the castle courtyard leading two saddled horses. 'There's no-one here,' he called softly.

Ashka and Paul hurried out of a doorway. Paul was disguised in a servant's uniform and carried a sack containing the fireworks. Ashka and Gryvon mounted their horses.

'Where's my horse?' Paul asked.

Gryvon smirked. 'Servants walk.'

'I don't want to get there tomorrow,' Ashka said sharply. 'Paul will ride with you.'

Gryvon grudgingly hauled Paul onto the horse behind him then trotted after Ashka.

As a guard hurried to open the gate, Riana crept onto a balcony overlooking the court-yard. She saw the three figures riding out of the castle and recognised Paul. Before she could do anything, the guard closed the gate.

Correon was fast asleep when a pair of fingers pinched his nostrils shut. He snorted loudly, and his eyes flew open. He was shocked to see Riana standing over him. He opened his mouth to call for help but Riana put her hand over it.

'Ashka took Paul from his cell and hid him in a cellar,' she said quickly. 'She's been getting him to make gunpowder. He's in danger. You've got to help him!'

Grumbling to himself, Correon threw on a warm cloak and followed Riana through the castle to the cellar. Holding a lighted torch, Riana showed Correon the iron pot on the table. 'That's what he made the gunpowder in. Look.' She scraped a few grains of black powder from the bottom of the pot and dropped them into the torch flame. They flared brightly.

'Where has Ashka gone?' Correon asked.

'I'm not telling unless you take me with
you.'

'You'll do as I say!'

'No, I won't,' Riana said defiantly.

Correon shook his head. 'You're the most
stubborn person I've ever met.'

Riana smiled. 'You should meet my mother,
Spellbinder.'

The sun was well up as Correon rode out of the
castle. He was wearing his power suit. Riana
followed him on foot.

'I haven't been outside the castle in years,'
Correon said, riding slowly so he could look
around.

'We must hurry, Spellbinder,' Riana said.

Correon drew his horse to a halt and looked
down at her. 'Alright, you're out. Where's
Ashka?'

'I'm coming too. Help me up.' Riana held
out her hand. Correon glared at her but she
held his gaze. Correon relented and helped her
up onto the horse.

'Do you know where the ruins are?' Riana

asked.

Correon spurred his horse away from the castle.

'Have a good time, darling,' Mrs Muggleton said to Katrina. 'We're very proud of you. Here's the money for the camp.'

Katrina guiltily took the money and got out of the car with her overnight bag. As her mother drove away, Alex appeared from behind a tree.

Katrina stared at him. 'Why are you dressed like that?'

He was wearing a cardigan, glasses and had his hair slicked back. 'I don't want anyone to recognise me. Great, you've got my money.' He reached for it but Katrina held it away.

'Nick off, that's my mum's money.'

'What about my costs?'

A bus pulled up outside the school and Mr Byrne, the literature camp leader, got off.

'Deanna and Nathan?'

Alex snatched the money from Katrina and

smiled at Mr Byrne. 'That's us.'

Mr Byrne checked his clipboard. 'You're all paid up, Deanna. Nathan, you still owe $100.'

Alex groaned and handed over the money. Katrina smirked.

'Let us take the best and largest shields,' Mr Byrne declaimed loudly, waving his pen in the air like a sword, 'put blazing helmets on our heads and go forward. Onward to Troy!'

The students on the bus clapped. Mr Byrne took a bow and got back on the bus.

'What a dipstick,' Alex whispered to Katrina as they got on. He spotted a seat next to an attractive girl and dived into it. Katrina took the seat behind them. 'Hi, I'm Alex,' he said to the girl.

Katrina thumped him in the back. 'He's Nathan,' she said pointedly. 'I'm Deanna.'

'I'm Skye,' the girl said.

'I'll bet you're not an air-head,' Alex joked. 'Get it? Air? Sky?'

Skye didn't laugh. The bus drove off.

'Well ... er ... read any good books lately?' Alex asked Skye.

'I absolutely adored *The Iliad*.'

'I haven't got around to that yet.'

'But it's required reading for the camp,' Skye told him. 'We've all got to read from our favourite passages.'

Alex turned to Katrina. 'I'll never get away with this,' he moaned.

Correon drew his horse to a halt by a pile of fallen masonry. Riana looked up. The grey stone ruins of an ancient castle loomed over them.

'This was a Spellbinder castle once,' Correon said. 'It was destroyed by the Marauders during the Darkness.'

He and Riana dismounted and picked their way through the ruins to a part of the castle that was still intact. They peered through a gap in the wall.

In a courtyard below, Ashka and Gryvon were watching Paul place a firework on a pile of rocks. Paul lit the fuse and stepped back. The fuse spluttered then the firework exploded with a small bang and a puff of smoke.

'That wouldn't scare a baby, let alone a Marauder,' Ashka snapped at Paul.

'I'll try a bigger one.'

Paul lit the fuse of a larger firework. Ashka snatched it from him and dropped it into the sack of fireworks.

'Run!' Paul yelled.

He and Gryvon scrambled away and threw themselves to the ground. Ashka wedged the sack between some blocks of stone. The sack exploded with a huge roar, throwing rock and debris high into the air.

'That's what I was hoping for,' Ashka said, looking at the crater made by the explosion.

'Now will you help me get home?' Paul asked.

'Soon. But first I want to know more about this world you come from.'

'I'm not telling you anything else,' Paul said stubbornly. 'And I'm not making any more gunpowder unless you help me get home.'

'It doesn't matter, Paul. I have made my own gunpowder.' Gryvon opened his sack and showed Paul the black powder inside. Paul grabbed the burning torch and thrust it into the sack. Gryvon threw himself to the ground and covered his head with his hands, waiting for the explosion. Nothing happened. Gryvon looked up at Paul, who was grinning. 'You tricked me!' He leaped angrily to his feet and was about to hit Paul when Correon's voice came from Ashka's Eyestone.

'Ashka, this is Correon. Where are you?'

Ashka took out her Eyestone and opened it. 'Out riding, Regent.'

In their hiding place, Correon winked at Riana as he spoke into his Eyestone. 'I need to speak to you immediately. It will be to your benefit.'

Ashka closed her Eyestone and turned to Gryvon. 'Tie up the boy and wait for me.' She mounted her horse and rode off.

Gryvon dragged Paul to his feet. 'The truth is, Paul,' he gloated, 'you're never going home.'

'Yes he is.'

Gryvon whirled around and saw Correon and Riana climbing through the ruins.

'Paul, your knowledge is too dangerous for

this world,' Correon said. 'We have to get you home.'

Gryvon turned and ran; Paul went after him. As he crossed the crater left by the exploding fireworks, the ground gave way. With a cry of dismay, Paul disappeared from sight.

He landed with a crash on a stone floor, and clouds of dust billowed up. The air smelt of decay. He coughed and looked around. A beam of light from the hole above showed Paul that he was in a large underground vault.

Something white gleamed in the sunlight: Paul realised that it was a human skeleton. He backed away and stumbled into another. Paul looked frantically around and discovered he was surrounded by skeletons. He screamed.

Secrets of the Spellbinders

A rope dropped through the hole in the ceiling of the vault and Riana slid easily to the floor. Paul was cowering against the stone wall, staring fearfully at the skeletons.

'They're only dead people,' Riana scoffed. 'What are you frightened of?'

'I just hurt myself when I fell,' Paul lied, getting to his feet.

He and Riana looked around the gloomy vault. More skeletons lay on decayed beds and couches. Some were wearing the rotted remains of power suits.

'Regent, come down,' Riana called. 'You've got to see this.' She lit candles around the walls of the vault as Gryvon slid down the rope. Correon followed awkwardly after him and looked around.

'Spellbinders!' he gasped. 'They must have

189

been here since the time of the Darkness.' He went to a desk where a skeleton sat slumped over a thick, octagonal book. He carefully opened it and leafed through the pages. 'These are plans for constructing a power suit,' he said with growing amazement. 'And a flying ship. See? These are the Spellbinder secrets I've been searching for. We can build new suits and ships!'

As Correon kept reading, Paul wandered around the vault, examining the rusted machinery and old books filling the corners and shelves. He hesitantly touched a skeleton. It fell apart, the white bones clattering on the floor.

'Careful,' Correon snapped. 'These are my ancestors.'

'Why are they down here?'

'I don't know.'

Correon noticed a skeleton at another desk. It had collapsed over an open journal and a pen was still clutched in its bony fingers. Correon blew the dust off the pages and began to read out loud. '"The others are all dead of hunger and despair. Now I have finished this account of the disaster, I too may rest. If any survive the Darkness, read these words and learn. Do not repeat our mistake."'

'What mistake?' Paul asked.

'I don't know.' Correon turned to the beginning of the journal.

'Shouldn't we get going before Ashka finds out you tricked her?' Paul asked anxiously.

'I can't leave now. This find is much too important.'

'I'll go and keep watch,' Riana said. She shinned up the rope and out of the vault.

'Impossible!' Correon suddenly cried. 'The fools! It was the Spellbinders themselves who caused the Darkness, not the Marauders. The old Spellbinders were trying to increase their powers but something went wrong. Listen.'

Paul joined Correon at the desk as he read from the book: 'Moments after the experiment began, the earth convulsed. Cracks appeared in the ground and mountains of fire arose.'

'Earthquakes and volcanoes,' Paul exclaimed. 'That's why this world looks so different from mine.'

Behind them, Gryvon crept to the rope and began to climb it.

'The sky was black with clouds and the sun disappeared,' Correon read on. 'The trees began to die.'

'It sounds like a nuclear winter.'

Correon gave Paul a puzzled look.

'In my world, people learnt to turn fireworks into bombs,' Paul explained. 'One bomb can destroy a whole castle. A nuclear bomb is a million times more powerful.'

'Madness!' Correon exclaimed.

'If enough of them ever went off, they would blow so much dirt into the air it would block out the sun. There would be a winter that lasted for years. All the trees and animals would die. The old Spellbinders must have caused something like that.'

'They were arrogant fools. Like Ashka.'

'Ashka already knows how to turn fireworks into bombs,' Paul reminded Correon.

'Then she must not be allowed to learn the secret of making gunpowder. We must find a way of sending you back to your world.'

This was exactly what Paul had been hoping

to hear. 'We have to go to the Summoning Tower at Clayhill,' he said, 'That's where I arrived.'

Gryvon reached the hole in the ceiling and climbed out. He started pulling up the rope. Falling dirt made Paul and Correon look up.

'Put it back, Gryvon!' Correon ordered.

Gryvon smirked at Correon as he pulled the rope out of reach. He ran to his horse and leaped into the saddle. As he started to ride away, Riana's bolas whirled through the air and wrapped around him. Gryvon struggled to get free but Riana yanked on the cord and pulled him off the horse. She bound the winded Apprentice and ran back to the hole over the vault. Below her, Paul was perched precariously on Correon's back, trying to climb out. Correon collapsed and they crashed to the ground. Clouds of dust billowed around them and Correon started coughing. Riana laughed. 'Need some help?' she asked and threw down the rope.

Ashka strode into the Regents' chamber and bowed to Lukan and Marna. She looked around the chamber, puzzled. 'I was expecting to meet Regent Correon.'

'Correon left the castle this morning,' Lukan said. 'It's very odd. He hasn't been outside the castle in years.'

There was a crackle of static as Correon's voice came from the Eyestone on the chamber wall. 'Marna, Lukan, I've found the boy.'

'Good,' Lukan said. 'Bring him back to the castle.'

'No. I'm sending him back to his world. His knowledge is too dangerous for us. When you see what I have found, you will understand why.'

'We demand that you bring him back,' Lukan roared.

'Lukan, it's Gryvon! They're going to Cl ...' Gryvon's voice was cut off. The Regents waited but the Eyestone remained silent.

'I think I know where Correon and the boy are,' Ashka said. 'Let me bring them back.'

Lukan and Marna nodded their assent.

Paul and Riana splashed across a creek which ran through a peaceful meadow. Paul felt relaxed for the first time in days. He was finally on his way home. He looked back as Correon coughed. The old Spellbinder did not look well. Gryvon stumbled along behind Correon's horse, tied to the saddle by a rope. Suddenly a loud·throbbing filled the air.

'Ashka,' Gryvon yelled.

A flying ship appeared above the tree-tops. Correon spurred his horse forward and they took shelter beneath the branches of a tree. Paul and Riana held Gryvon tightly until the flying· ship moved away. Then Correon's Eyestone started to beep loudly. The flying ship turned back towards them.

'Ashka has activated my Eyestone,' Correon said with dismay. 'She'll find us.'

'Can't you turn it off?' Paul asked desperately.

'No.'

'We have to get rid of it. Give it to me and I'll lead them away from you.'

'Don't be ridiculous. You're the one she's after.'

'Give it to me,' Riana demanded.

Correon handed her the Eyestone. Riana

smashed it on a rock. The beeping stopped. Correon looked at Riana with admiration. 'Clever girl.'

To Gryvon's dismay, the flying ship turned and flew away.

The literature students were gathered on the lawn of the Mount Lara school camp, listening rapturously to Mr Byrne as he lectured on Greek literature. Katrina sat at the back of the group with Alex, who was yawning. 'Homer's *Iliad* is full of suffering and pain,' Mr Byrne was explaining. 'Young men die, women and children lose husbands and fathers. But the Gods, exempt from pain, look on.'

'I'm suffering,' Alex whispered to Katrina, 'and he's the pain.'

'Let's start with something simple,' Mr Byrne continued. 'What setting did Homer chose for his great human tragedy?'

'The war between the Trojans and the Greeks?' Skye answered.

'Come on the Greeks!' Alex cheered, hoping

to get her attention.

Skye and the other students turned and stared at him. 'You're not supposed to be Greek, *Nathan*,' Katrina whispered.

'Since you've picked sides, Nathan,' Mr Byrne said, 'you can begin reading from the start of Book One.'

Alex groaned and looked at Katrina for help but there wasn't a thing she could do. Trying to hide his panic, Alex opened the book. He began to read, stumbling through the text and mispronouncing all the long words. '"Sing, goddess, of the anger of Achilleus, son of Peleus, the accursed anger which brought uncounted anguish on the Achaians."' Alex heard students tittering and stopped reading.

'Nathan wasn't feeling too well on the bus, sir,' Katrina improvised. 'He gets car sickness.'

Alex pretended to gag and the students within spewing distance quickly moved away.

'I'll take him to the toilets.' Katrina helped Alex up and led him behind the buildings.

'Thanks,' Alex said.

'Let's go up to the cave now,' Katrina suggested.

They crept into the bush and made their way up the trail. 'What are we looking for?' Alex asked as they approached the cave.

'I don't know. Let's go through what happened.' Katrina stood in front of the cave. 'Paul was standing here when he disappeared. The power surge came down the cable from there. And this whole area is surrounded by magnetic rock.

'So?'

'I don't know!'

'Great!' Alex sat on the rocks by the cave, took out a small radio and tuned in a football game.

Katrina paced the area, looking for clues. The tinny sound of the football commentary started to annoy her. 'Alex, please. I'm trying to think.'

'But my team's in the semis.'

'Turn it off.'

'If they win, they're into the Grand Final ... '

'Alex!'

Katrina made a grab for the radio but Alex clung onto it. As they struggled, Alex's fingers moved the tuning dial. There was the sound of static, then Ashka's voice crackled from the radio: '... report any sighting of Regent Correon travelling with a boy called Paul.'

Alex stared at Katrina in amazement. 'Did she say "Paul"?'

'The boy is about fifteen years old with dark hair,' Ashka continued. 'He speaks with a strange voice.'

'It is Paul,' Katrina said excitedly.

'If sighted, report to the Spellbinders immediately. Do not approach them.' There was another crackle of static and then the radio went silent.

'What's a Spellbinder?' Alex asked.

'Who cares?' Katrina replied. 'They use radio. Paul is in a parallel world and we can prove it exists.'

'If we can hear them,' Alex said, 'maybe they can hear us. If we had a radio transmitter ...'

'Where are we going to get a transmitter?'

'They had walkie-talkies last time we were at the camp.'

'I don't know why people say you're stupid.'

'Who says I'm stupid?'

Katrina laughed. 'We'd better get back before we're missed.'

A campfire glowed in a thick grove of trees. Correon slept fitfully beside it, covered with skins. Gryvon sat unhappily against the trunk of a tree, bound and gagged. Riana noticed Paul staring despondently into the fire. 'What's the matter?' she asked

'I was just wondering how Dad's coping with me being gone. It was bad enough when Mum died.'

'Don't worry. Correon will find a way to get you home.'

'What if he doesn't?'

Riana didn't have an answer. Correon coughed in his sleep and Riana felt his forehead. 'He's very cold.' Paul wrapped his cloak around Correon.

Gryvon mumbled loudly under his gag. Paul went over and loosened it. 'I'm hungry,' Gryvon wailed.

'So are we,' Paul told him. 'And if you don't behave yourself, we might think about eating you.'

Gryvon gulped. As Paul tightened the gag, the familiar throbbing of a flying ship shattered the stillness of the night. Gryvon quickly rolled towards the fire and kicked a pile of leaves and branches into the flames. The fire flared and a shower of sparks flew upwards.

Riana smothered the fire with a cloak as Paul shook Correon awake. They stared at the flying ship hovering above the trees.

'Ashka knows we're down here,' Gryvon gloated.

'They can't land,' Correon croaked. 'But they'll send men to find us. We have to go.' Correon struggled to his feet and Paul and Riana helped him on to the horse. As he settled in the saddle, he convulsed in a fit of coughing.

'We're not far from Clayhill,' Riana told Paul. 'Our Healer could help him.'

'But we have to get to the Summoning Tower.'

Correon coughed again. 'Paul,' Riana pleaded, 'he's not well.'

'All right!'

The door to the camp storeroom creaked open and Alex and Katrina slipped inside. Katrina groped for the light-switch and turned it on. 'If there's a radio in the camp, it'll be in here,' she said. 'Did you bring the book?'

Alex held up a copy of *The Iliad*.

'Start reading. If anyone comes in, we're just studying for tomorrow.'

As Katrina started searching through the jumble of equipment in the storeroom, Alex began reading out loud. '"Agamemnon stabbed him in the forehead with his sharp spear, and it went through the bone and all his brains were spattered inside." Gross! Hey, this is good stuff!'

'I think it's stupid. All those men killing each other over a girl.'

'Well, you don't have to worry: no man's

ever going to go to war over you.'

Katrina shot Alex a look that could have stripped paint.

'Sorry, Katrina. Any luck?'

'No. Keep reading.'

'"Agamemnon, lord of men, left them as they lay ..."'

'Eureka!' Katrina cried. Inside a cupboard was a box containing two-way radios. Katrina took one and turned the power-switch. 'It doesn't work,' she said in dismay.

At the back of the cupboard, Alex saw some batteries in a recharger. He grabbed one. 'Now it will.'

'Let's go up to the cave and try it.'

As they turned to leave, Mr Byrne walked in. Katrina quickly hid the radio behind her back and Alex pocketed the battery. 'What are you two doing in here?' Mr Byrne asked suspiciously.

'Preparing for tomorrow's class, sir.' Alex held up his book but Mr Byrne did not look convinced.

'I was quite explicit about the rules for this camp,' he said severely. 'Boys and girls are not to fraternise after dark.'

'We weren't fraternising, sir. We were reading *The Iliad*.'

'I'm sorry, but I'll have to inform your parents tomorrow.' He took out his notebook and pencil. 'Nathan, isn't it?'

'Yes, sir, Nathan Jones,' Alex replied.

Mr Byrne made a note. 'And Deanna McDougall?' Katrina nodded.

'I'm very disappointed in you both. Come along, Deanna, I'll escort you back to your dormitory. Nathan, I'll expect you to be in bed by the time I get back.'

Katrina managed to keep the radio hidden as Mr Byrne escorted her out.

Maran sat at the table in the cottage, shaping a lump of red clay into a pot. Jal and Arla sat close by, copying her handiwork.

'The Summoner asked after Riana again today,' Maran said casually to Bron, who was brooding by the fire-pit.

'What did you tell him?'

'Just what you told me. That she went hunting.'

'But she's been gone three days,' said a worried Arla. 'What if she's had an accident?'

A blast of cold air made everyone turn. Riana stood in the open doorway. Maran gave a cry of relief. 'We've been worried sick. Where have you been?'

'To the Spellbinders' castle.' Riana's family gaped.

Then Paul came through the door. 'Hello Maran, Bron.'

Before anyone could speak, Correon followed Paul in. Maran fell to her knees.

'Spellbinder!' she pleaded. 'My daughter is a good girl. She can be wild and stubborn but ...'

'Don't be afraid,' Correon said gently. 'I am in your daughter's debt.'

His thin body was racked by another coughing fit.

'He needs the Healer,' Riana said and ran out.

Paul and Maran helped Correon to the fire. 'Can I make you some tea?' Maran asked nervously. 'Are you hungry? What do Spellbinders eat?'

Correon laughed, then started coughing again.

Riana returned with the Healer, who examined Correon and then prepared a mixture of herbs and powders in a bowl. She set it smouldering and Correon bent over it to inhale the fumes. After a while, he looked up and smiled. 'These herbs are powerful. I feel better already.'

As he inhaled again, Jal crept to his side. 'Can you do magic?' the boy asked.

'I am a Spellbinder. Of course I can do magic. Watch.' Correon produced two small metal balls. He put one in the palm of his right hand and held the other ball above it. Slowly, he brought the balls closer. The one in his palm suddenly jumped up and clung to the other. Jal and Arla gasped with surprise at the magnetic effect.

'Jumping balls,' Jal said.

'Take them. They will bring you good luck.' Correon gave Jal and Arla a ball each and patted their heads. Maran smiled at Bron. She still couldn't believe it. A Spellbinder was staying in her home.

The sun had just risen as Maran carried a tray of her pots into the barn. As she put down the tray she heard a sound and saw movement under a pile of hides. She used a pitchfork to lift them. Gryvon lay underneath, where Paul and Riana had hidden him the night before. He was bound and gagged. Maran quickly untied the gag.

'Release me now,' Gryvon barked, 'or I'll make sure that Riana is banished.'

Maran quickly got to work on the ropes.

'Where is Paul?' Gryvon asked.

'I don't know. He and Riana left early with Regent Correon.'

'So why didn't the Greeks just pack up and go home?' Mr Byrne asked his students. It was just after breakfast on the second day of the camp.

'Because they were Greek,' Alex suggested.

Some of the students laughed.

'I'm serious: the Greeks were proud warriors. They had to stay at Troy for their honour.'

'Very good, Nathan. Pride and honour are at the crux of this story.'

Alex noticed that Skye was looking at him in an I-might-have-been-wrong-about-you sort of way. He didn't see Katrina trying to attract his attention from behind a tree. 'And, of course, the Greeks would never give up a beautiful girl without a fight,' he continued.

He looked at Skye, who rewarded him with a smile in return. So this is what love feels like, Alex thought. Then a pine cone hit him in the back of the head. Alex looked around and saw Katrina beckoning from behind the tree.

'Sir, could I be excused for a minute?' he asked.

'Make it quick, Nathan. We value your comments.'

Alex got up. He swaggered past Skye, then headed into the trees. 'Can't we wait until after this class?' he asked Katrina. 'I'm doing really well.'

'We came up here to find Paul.'

'I know. But I stayed up all night reading. I never finished a book before. It's fun.'

'I'm glad *you* had fun,' Katrina said crossly. 'I sat outside your dormitory for half the night waiting for you to come out.'

'I couldn't. Byrne was sleeping by the door. Why didn't you go up to the cave on your own?'

'Because you had the battery.'

'Oh, right.' Alex guiltily removed the battery from his pocket and Katrina inserted it into the radio. She pressed the talk button.

'Hello?' she said eagerly. 'My name's Katrina. I'm trying to contact the Spellbinders. Can anyone hear me?'

There was no answer.

'Maybe it only works if we're up at the cave,' Alex suggested.

Paul, Riana and Correon stood at the base of the Summoning Tower.

'This is where I came through,' Paul said. 'In my world, electricity jumped from the power lines and came down the cable. There was a huge flash. When I could see again, I was standing here.' He pointed to the iron stand near the base of the tower. It was topped by a metal dish. 'There was energy sparking between the top of the tower and this dish. When I knocked the Eyestone off it, the energy doorway, or whatever it was, closed.'

Correon nodded thoughtfully. 'I think that when the Summoner used his Eyestone, the energy in this world must have connected with the energy in yours. That's what opened the doorway to your world. Let's see if we can make it happen again.'

'But I smashed your Eyestone,' Riana said.

'I may not need one. Paul, wait by the dish. Riana, stand back.'

Riana gave Paul's hand a quick squeeze for luck and moved away. Correon took up a position midway between the tower and the stand. He struck his wrists together, energising his power suit, then pointed one arm at the top of the tower and the other at the stand.

Energy began crackling around the tower. It flashed towards Correon, enveloped his power suit and shot from his outstretched hand to the dish. Paul watched eagerly but there was no sign of the energy doorway.

'It won't work without the cable in my world,' he said despondently.

'I'll try increasing the power flow. Paul, you'd better move away.'

As Paul hurried to join Riana, Correon energised his suit once more. A massive surge of power flashed from the tower, wrapped around Correon and hit the dish. The air nearby began to ripple.

'It's working!' Paul cried.

Katrina and Alex reached the top of the trail and stopped. Energy was rippling in the air in front of the cave. Katrina ran forward.

'Be careful,' Alex called. He joined Katrina a few metres from the energy curtain. As they watched, the curtain became transparent and they could see the vague outline of a human figure on the other side.

'There's someone there!' Katrina said excitedly.

Alex stared at the figure, recognition growing. 'Paul?' he yelled. 'Paul!'

Correon stood between the tower and stand, struggling to maintain the massive power flow. His face contorted with the effort, and smoke began to rise from his overheated power suit.

Paul stared through the rippling energy curtain. 'There are people there,' he said to Riana. 'Hello!'

Paul thought he heard a reply but it was too faint to be sure. The energy curtain suddenly flickered.

'I can't maintain the power flow!' Correon gasped.

'But it's nearly open!' Paul yelled. 'Just a few seconds longer.'

But the strain was too much. With a grunt of pain, Correon collapsed. To Paul's dismay, the energy curtain faded.

'What's happening?' Alex asked as the rippling energy disappeared.

'Paul, can you hear me?' Katrina yelled into the radio. 'Hello. Is anyone there?'

All they could hear was static.

'Maybe we're on the wrong frequency,' Alex suggested.

Katrina moved the channel selector. 'Hello, can anyone hear me?'

Paul and Riana crouched by the old Spellbinder, who lay motionless on the ground.

'Correon?' Paul whispered.

Correon groaned but his eyes remained closed.

'I'll go back to Clayhill and get help.' Riana ran to the trail and disappeared.

Paul took off his cloak and put it under Correon's head, hoping the old man would be alright. He heard a noise and looked around.

Gryvon, the Summoner and two men from the village were standing behind him. Gryvon smiled triumphantly as the men dragged Paul to his feet.

'Get away from him,' Riana cried. She stepped out from behind a rock, whirling her bolas.

'Put those down!' Gryvon ordered.

Riana ignored him.

'You dare to disobey an Apprentice?' Gryvon barked.

Riana held her ground. Gryvon and the Summoner stepped towards her. A power-bolt exploded at their feet. They turned and saw Correon standing unsteadily.

'Leave them alone,' Correon ordered.

The men let go of Paul and fell to their knees. The Summoner bowed nervously. Gryvon was furious. 'Father, you must report this to the other Regents.'

'I'm sorry, Regent Correon,' the Summoner said.

He placed his Eyestone in the dish on the stand but before he could open it, Correon hurled another bolt. The Eyestone exploded.

The Summoner fell to the ground, quaking with terror. Gryvon realised he had lost, and slowly sank to his knees.

'Riana, fetch my horse,' Correon said. Riana hurried away.

'We can't leave now,' Paul protested.

'We have to,' Correon said. 'Ashka will guess where we are.'

Riana returned with the horse. Paul and Riana helped Correon mount.

'Don't try to follow us,' Correon ordered. He wheeled his horse around and rode away from the tower. Paul and Riana hurried after him.

As soon as they were out of sight, Gryvon turned to one of his father's men. 'You,' he barked. 'Run to Rivertown and tell the Summoner there what has happened. Ask him to tell the Spellbinder Ashka where I am, so she can come and get me. In a flying ship we'll soon catch them.'

The man bowed and hurried away

Ashka was in her flying ship, searching for Paul and Correon from the air, when Alex's voice crackled from her Eyestone.

'This is Big Daddy Alex calling all hot doggers in the parallel world. Do you copy?'

Ashka was so surprised by the outlandish words that she almost lost control of the ship.

'Come in, dudes, this is Big Al talking at ya.'

'Who is this?' Ashka demanded.

'We're looking for Paul Reynolds,' Katrina said into the radio. 'Who are you?'

'I am the Spellbinder Ashka. How are you able to speak through the Eyestone?'

Before Alex and Katrina could think of an answer, Mr Byrne strode out of the bush.

'Well, well, Deanna and Nathan together again.' He grabbed the radio from Katrina and spoke tersely into it. 'Whoever you are, this conversation is over.' He switched the radio off.

'Please, Mr Byrne,' Alex pleaded. 'We're looking for a missing friend.'

'We've made contact with a parallel world,' Katrina added.

'I've had enough of your lies,' Mr Byrne snapped. 'I've just been on the phone. The real

Deanna and Nathan are both at home. You two are in a lot of trouble.'

The sun was rising as Paul and Riana packed up their camp. Paul had passed a miserable night, wondering if he was ever going to get home.

'When are we going back to Clayhill?' he asked Correon.

'We can't risk it yet: Ashka will be searching for us.'

Paul couldn't hide his disappointment.

'Don't worry,' Correon promised. 'I'll find a way to get you home. But for now we have to hide.'

'Cheer up, Paul,' Riana said. 'At least you're getting to see more of our land.

'I'm not a tourist!' Paul stalked off through the trees.

Correon mounted his horse and he and Riana followed. When they caught up with Paul, he was standing on a riverbank, staring at the rusting bulk of another Summoning Tower. Piled at the base of the tower were red sacks of grain marked with the Spellbinders' sign, together with farming implements and a couple of sleds.

'What's all this doing here?' Riana asked.

'I don't know.' The Spellbinder dismounted and moved warily towards the tower. Paul and Riana followed. Suddenly, the air was filled with the whirring sound of bullroarers.

'Marauders!' Paul shouted.

'Don't be ridiculous,' Correon chuckled. 'I told you, the Spellbinders caused the Darkness. There's no such thing as Marauders.'

'Then what are they?' Riana asked, pointing.

Correon and Paul looked behind them. Dark shapes were moving among the trees. Their misshapen bodies appeared to be covered in leaves. They looked part vegetable, part animal. The creatures stepped into the sunlight and Correon found himself face to face with the Marauders.

The Labyrinth

The Marauders lumbered forward, sharp-edged bullroarers whirling in their hands. For creatures that weren't supposed to exist, Correon thought, they looked awfully real. 'Run for the trees,' he yelled. 'Go!'

Paul and Riana ran. Correon energised his power suit and threw a power-bolt. It blasted a hole in the ground in front of the Marauders. They turned and fled.

As Paul and Riana ran through the forest, a Marauder dropped from a tree and knocked Paul to the ground. He struggled to throw the hideous creature off. Riana pulled out her bolas and began to whirl them, trying to get a clear shot. A huge Marauder burst out of the bushes and grabbed her, pinning her arms to her sides.

'Let them go,' Correon commanded.

The Marauders turned to see the Spellbinder behind them. For a moment, no-one moved. Then two more Marauders leaped from a tree and dropped a net over Correon. He struggled under the thick mesh, unable to use his power suit. 'Release me,' he cried. 'I am a Spellbinder!'

The Marauders dragged Correon towards the river and hurled him off the bank. As he hit the water, there was a flash of light and a loud electrical crack.

Correon got to his feet, dripping wet. He pulled the net off and tried to energise his power suit. Nothing happened.

'Why doesn't he use the power suit?' Riana asked Paul.

'It must have shorted out: the water took away its power.'

One of the Marauders looked at Paul, then spoke. 'I know this one, Kurn. I met him in the castle. He was a prisoner.' The Marauder threw back the hood covering its head. Paul was amazed to see the face of Zander, the young toy-maker from Rivertown. The other Marauders began removing their hoods and a stunned Riana realised that the fearsome Marauders were really people in disguise.

'You were banished to the Wastelands,' Paul said to Zander in astonishment.

'The Marauders rescued me and took me to their camp. Now I'm a Marauder too.'

'We set a trap to steal an Eyestone and we've caught a Spellbinder instead,' Kurn, the big Marauder, said. 'Go after his horse. We may find a use for it. And take off his power suit.' The Marauders dragged Correon from the river and started stripping off the suit.

'Don't hurt him,' Paul begged.

'It's alright, boy,' Kurn said gently. 'You're not his slave anymore.'

'You don't understand,' Paul protested. 'He's trying to help us.'

'He's our enemy,' the big Marauder growled. 'For once, *we* will decide the fate of a Spellbinder. Tie him up.'

As the Marauders bound Correon's hands, power began crackling around the top of the Summoning Tower. A distant throbbing could be heard.

'A flying ship,' Zander shouted, pointing to

221

a small dot in the sky. 'Spellbinders!'

'It's Ashka,' warned Riana.

'Get the supplies,' Kurn yelled.

The Marauders ran to the Summoning Tower and began throwing the farming tools and sacks of grain on to the sleds. Zander realised the flying ship would reach the tower before they could get away. 'Kurn,' he called. 'We'll have to leave the supplies and run.'

'I'm not leaving the food,' Kurn snapped. 'The children are starving. Hurry.'

'Wait,' Paul shouted, 'the Summoning Tower provides energy to the flying ship. If you pull it down, the ship will fall out of the sky.'

Kurn ignored Paul and kept working.

'He knows things, Kurn,' Zander said urgently. 'He knows about flying.'

Kurn looked up at the approaching flying ship. It was too late to run. 'Give me that chain,' he ordered.

Zander picked up a long iron chain from amongst the farming tools and handed it to Kurn. There was a hook on the end. Kurn swung the chain around his head and let it go.

With a loud clang, the hook caught the framework of the tower. The Marauders grabbed the chain and pulled. Paul and Riana joined them but the tower was built to take the weight of a flying ship. It didn't even move.

'It's no use,' Kurn yelled. 'Run!'

The Marauders dropped the chain. It fell across the cables connecting the Eyestone dish to the tower. Sparks flew and there was a loud electrical crack.

'Look,' Riana cried.

The flying ship was spiralling out of control. It disappeared behind a hill and there was the sound of a distant crash. The Marauders cheered.

'Well done, boy,' Kurn said, slapping Paul on the back. 'But now that you've seen what we are, you must both come with us.'

'You'll be safe,' Zander promised. 'The Marauders aren't really monsters.'

'Let's get moving,' Kurn ordered.

The Marauders finished loading the sleds and began dragging them into the forest. One of them pulled Correon along by the rope binding his hands.

'Shall we make a run for it?' Riana whispered to Paul.

Paul shook his head. 'I'm not going anywhere without Correon.'

As they reluctantly joined the Marauders, Paul looked back at the tower. Energy still sparked down the chain.

'It's shorting out just like the cable Alex and I rigged,' he told Riana excitedly. 'Maybe I can use a chain like that to get home.'

Alex waved as Katrina came through the school gates. She ignored him. He ran after her. 'Katrina! What's up?'

She kept walking. 'I'm supposed to stay away from you. Dad blew his top over what happened at the camp. I tried to tell them about Paul and speaking to the Spellbinder on the radio but they think I'm just making it up.'

'What did you expect?'

Katrina shrugged. 'What did you tell your
parents?' she asked.

'That I went on the camp because I fancied you.'

Katrina's jaw dropped.

'Pop was proud of me,' Alex said, grinning. 'He wants to know when he's going to meet my girlfriend. Want to come round for dinner?'

'I'm not your girlfriend,' Katrina snapped.

She walked away but Alex kept up with her. 'Come on, Katrina, it was a joke. Listen, the camp wasn't a total disaster. Now we know for sure that Paul's in a parallel world.'

'But who's going to believe us? It's too fantastic.'

'What if we could get Paul's dad to listen to the Spellbinders?' Alex asked.

'We'd have to get him up to the cave,' Katrina reminded him. 'The radio only picks up the Spellbinders there.'

'So what are we going to do? We can't give up now.'

'I'm all out of ideas, Alex. It's your turn.' She walked off.

'Lovers' tiff?'

Alex turned and saw Nathan behind him.

'These cross-cultural romances are always difficult,' Nathan sympathised. 'Don't give up. I'm relying on you.'

'What are you talking about?' Alex said irritably.

'I'm writing a romantic novel about you two, remember? I want to know everything that happened at the literature camp.'

Alex was about to tell Nathan where he could stuff his novel when he noticed his T-shirt. It was printed with the logo of a radio communications system.

'Great T-shirt, Nathan,' he said enthusiastically. 'Where d'ya get it?'

'My dad sells this stuff.'

'Do you know anything about radios?'

'Sure. I work in the shop after school.'

Alex put his arm around Nathan's shoulder as if he was an old friend. 'After what happened at the camp, Katrina's mum won't let her talk to me on the phone,' he told Nathan sadly. 'And my pop won't let me see her. He's sending me up to the mountains on the weekends to help Uncle Dimitri with his chickens. I'll be up to my armpits in manure all weekend. I really love her, mate.' Alex started to sob and buried his face in his hands.

'It's OK, mate,' Nathan said, patting him on the back. 'How can I help?'

Alex grinned beneath his hands, then sobbed tragically. 'If I could just speak to Katrina on the weekends, I could bear it. I was wondering if you could help me get some kind of radio system or something.'

'I don't know. That equipment's pretty expensive.'

'But think, Nathe,' Alex said, pretending to wipe away tears, 'I can record everything we say to each other. You can use it in your book.'

Nathan's eyes lit up.

Battered from their flying ship crash, Ashka and Gryvon cautiously emerged from the trees and approached the Summoning Tower. Gryvon pointed to a torn grain sack and an abandoned sled. 'Marauders!'

Ashka saw the chain hanging from the Summoning Tower. Energy was still sparking down it. 'They have discovered how to bring down our flying ships,' she said in horror.

She used a long branch to pull the chain off the tower. The sparking stopped. As Ashka dropped the branch, she noticed the distinctive footprints of Paul's runners in the soft earth. 'Those are Paul's footprints,' she said, examining the ground. 'And a horse has been here.'

'The Marauders have captured Correon,' Gryvon said in dismay. 'We must inform the Regents.'

'Correon isn't important,' Ashka snapped. 'What if the Marauders force Paul to give them the secret of the gunpowder?'

Gryvon was horrified. He looked at the tracks left by the loaded sleds. 'We can follow them.'

Ashka nodded and they followed the trail into the forest.

As the day wore on, the Marauder raiding party dragged their laden sleds up a steep, rocky trail. They were deep in the mountains.

'So your clothes are just to scare people off so they don't fight?' Paul asked Zander.

'It was Kurn's idea. The Spellbinders always blame the Marauders for everything bad that happens. But no-one had ever seen one.'

'So you pretend to be Marauders,' Riana said. 'That's clever.'

'Are all the Marauders people who have been banished?' Paul asked Kurn.

'Not all. Some just hated the Spellbinders and ran away.'

'Why would anyone hate the Spellbinders?' Correon asked.

'Because we are punished if we say or do anything other than what you tell us,' Zander said heatedly.

'We only do it for your own good,' Correon replied.

'My village had fields full of rocks,' Kurn said quietly. 'Our tools kept breaking so I built a big blade that could be pulled by an ox. It worked well but the Spellbinders destroyed it. For that I was banished to the Wastelands!'

'He ate insects to stay alive and managed to crawl back to the mountains,' Zander proudly explained.

'I'm sorry, but the law is the law,' Correon

insisted. 'You cannot have civilisation without laws.'

'One day there will be enough of us to defeat the Spellbinders and then we will make our own laws,' Kurn said angrily. 'I'm going to have to blindfold you now. I can't risk the Spellbinders finding out where our camp is.'

For what seemed like hours, Paul, Riana and Correon stumbled along the trail as the Marauders led them blindfolded further into the mountains. Paul was aware of being pushed through a narrow rock opening.

'You can remove the blindfolds now,' Kurn said.

Paul, Riana and Correon thankfully took the bindings from their eyes and blinked. They were standing at the junction of a maze of passages running between water-worn rocks. The sky was visible through a thin crack high overhead.

'Stay close,' Kurn warned. 'If you get lost in here, you'll never be found.'

He led the way, moving surely through the labyrinth of passages. Paul quickly lost all sense of direction.

Eventually, they emerged into a large clearing surrounded by a high wall of rock. It was the Marauder camp. Patchworks of canvas, animal hides and grain sacks stretched between the rocks to create dwellings that were half-tent, half-cave. A wooden windmill sat on the ridge surrounding the camp, pumping water from a well into a tank. Hollowed-out tree trunks formed an aqueduct which carried water around the camp. Children played in the mud and music could be heard. The people were thin and dressed in rags but the camp had an air of vitality.

A woman and a young girl ran to Kurn and hugged him. Cailin and Rinske were Kurn's wife and daughter.

'Did you get any food?' Cailin asked eagerly.

Kurn grinned and pointed to the sleds piled with sacks. 'And a Spellbinder,' he said.

Cailin and Rinske stared at Correon in fear. 'Don't worry,' Kurn reassured them. 'Without his suit, he's just a harmless old man. We'll decide what to do with him tonight. Take care of him, Tark.'

An older Marauder pulled Correon away

from Paul and shoved him towards a cave.

'Don't hurt him,' Paul shouted.

'That's the boy from Clayhill,' Cailin exclaimed. 'The one who drove us off with the magic firepots. He's a friend of the Spellbinders.'

'He was their prisoner,' Zander said in Paul's defence. 'And he showed us how to bring down a flying ship.'

'Don't trust him,' Cailin urged. 'Put him with the Spellbinder.'

'Why?' Zander asked. 'He can't escape. He'd never find his way back through the labyrinth.'

'Without him we would not have the food,' Kurn added. 'Tonight, we will put the Spellbinder to trial. Then we will ask the boy about his magic. Now, let's unload the grain. Today, we eat!' The Marauders cheered and began to unload their booty into a dry cave.

'Why don't you grow your own food?' Riana asked as she helped Cailin carry a sack.

'We used to grow crops in the forest. But the Spellbinders destroyed them. The soil here is too thin so we have no choice but to steal.'

'But you're stealing from honest farmers,' Riana protested.

'We only take food meant for the Spellbinders,' Cailin explained, pointing to the Spellbinder signs on the red sacks.

'What will you do with Correon?' Paul asked.

'We'll take a vote,' Cailin replied.

'He's not a bad man.'

'He banished me for making a toy,' Zander said angrily.

Paul knew that Zander was right. Correon was as guilty of cruelty as the other Spellbinders. But he felt that Correon had changed. And he was the only hope Paul had of getting back to his own world.

Katrina hurried across the road towards Alex, who was waiting impatiently outside Nathan's shop.

'I was beginning to think you weren't coming,' he said.

'I nearly didn't,' Katrina admitted, looking

nervously up and down the street. 'If anyone who knows my parents sees me with you, I'll be grounded forever.'

'Chill out,' Alex said. 'This won't take long. All you have to do is pretend that you're hopelessly in love with me. It shouldn't be too hard.' He tried to look sexy.

'You are so up yourself,' Katrina told him.

'This isn't easy for me either, you know.'

'What's that supposed to mean?' Katrina snapped.

'Nothing,' Alex said with mock innocence. 'Look, are you coming or not?' He held out his hand. Katrina grudgingly took it and they went inside.

The shop was crammed from floor to ceiling with two-way radios, car alarms and electronic components. As Alex and Katrina came through the door, Nathan gave them a knowing smile from behind the counter. 'I'll take care of this,' he called to his father who was serving a customer at the other end of the shop.

Nathan pulled some boxes from under the counter and showed them to Alex and Katrina. 'Dad says you'll need a high-powered transmitter to communicate between the mountains and Katrina's house.'

'You told your dad about us?' Katrina asked in dismay.

'It's cool,' Nathan assured her. 'I told him it was for a school project. He says we can borrow the radios for a couple of weeks.'

'Nathan, you're brilliant,' Alex gushed. 'Your book's going to be a best-seller.'

Nathan beamed at the praise. 'I've already come up with the title: "Two-Way Love".'

'That's very creative, Nathan.' Katrina cooed.

Nathan opened one of the boxes and took out a two-way radio. 'These radios work just like a telephone,' he explained. 'We'll route the signals through some community repeater stations and ...'

'We don't need to know the technicalities,' Alex interrupted. 'We're in love.' He gave Katrina a gooey look. Katrina tried not to vomit.

'When will I get the tapes of your conversations?' Nathan asked excitedly.

'First thing on Monday,' Alex promised.

'How long do the batteries last?' Katrina asked.

'About six hours.'

'That won't be long enough,' she objected. 'Once Alex starts reading me his love poems he never stops.'

'Alex writes poems?' Nathan asked in amazement.

'Really long ones. It would be such a pity if the batteries ran out in the middle of one.'

Alex grinned. Katrina was really getting the hang of this. Nathan pointed to a display. 'You could run the radio off a solar cell.'

'Oh, Nathan,' Katrina simpered, 'our love powered by the energy of the sun—how romantic.'

Nathan couldn't help smiling. He knew his first novel was going to be a blockbuster.

An hour later, Alex and Katrina were unpacking the radio equipment in Alex's garage.

'We still have to figure out how to get the transmitter up to the cave,' Alex reminded

Katrina.

'Sorry,' she said, checking her watch, 'I've got to go.'

'But I need you to help me put this stuff together.'

'You can read,' Katrina said. 'Use the instruction manual.'

As she handed Alex the thick book, his brother drove into the garage. He got out of the car, carrying his mechanic's toolbox.

'Hi, Nick,' Alex called. 'How was work?'

'Good,' Nick mumbled, eyeing Katrina.

'Katrina,' Alex said. 'This is my brother, Nick.'

Nick winked at Katrina. 'Alex told me what youse got up to at the camp. So what's a foxy babe like you see in a loser like him?'

'He writes great poems. Ask him to read you some.'

Nick gaped at his brother. As he put his toolkit on the bench, he noticed the radio equipment. 'What's all that stuff?'

'I'm helping Katrina with a school project,' Alex lied. 'Can I use your tools?'

'If you put them back.' Nick picked up a rag.

He smeared his hands and face with oil as he went out.

'Why did he do that?' Katrina asked.

Alex shrugged. He opened Nick's toolbox and started looking for a screwdriver. There was a pink slip at the bottom. Alex took it out and read it.

'Oh no! Nick got fired from the garage,' he told Katrina. 'A month ago. What does he do every day? Pop's going to be really angry if he finds out.' And then he suddenly grinned. 'I wonder if Nick feels like a drive to the mountains tomorrow.'

The Marauder camp was lit by fires and torches. Kurn and Correon stood on a rock, listening to the tirade of angry words from the assembled Marauders.

'The Spellbinders have ruled our lives for too long,' Cailin yelled.

'We've only ever wanted what's best for you,' Correon argued.

'I've never seen a starving Spellbinder,' Tark jeered.

'We may have made mistakes,' Correon admitted. 'But we can undo them. Let me go back to the castle and ...'

'And tell the other Spellbinders where our camp is,' Cailin interrupted. 'So they can destroy us.'

'We should give him a taste of his own medicine,' a voice yelled. 'Banish him to the Wastelands!'

There were shouts of agreement. Paul rushed to Correon's side. 'Then you'll be as bad as the Spellbinders,' he yelled.

'Why do you defend him?' Zander asked. 'They were going to banish you.'

'It was Correon who helped me escape.'

'Why did he do that?' Kurn asked.

'I have knowledge the Spellbinders want.'

'What knowledge?'

'Paul, don't tell them,' Correon shouted.

Paul hesitated.

'If you won't tell us then we must sentence the Spellbinder,' Kurn said, turning back to the crowd. 'What will we do with him?'

'Banish him,' Tark yelled.

'Who agrees?' Kurn asked.

One by one, the Marauders raised their hands. Kurn nodded. 'Tomorrow, the Spellbinder goes to the Wastelands.'

Paul watched in dismay as Correon was dragged to the cave and thrown inside.

Back in Zander's shelter, Paul threw himself on to a pile of skins. 'If Correon is banished,' he said, 'I'll never get home.'

'Tell them about the gunpowder,' Riana urged. 'Then they'll let him go.'

'No! They'll use it to try and destroy the Spellbinders.'

'The Spellbinders are already trying to destroy us,' Zander said bitterly. 'Give us a chance to fight back.'

'Then there'll be a war.'

'What's a war?' Zander asked Paul.

'I'm sick of this,' Paul said. 'I just want to go home. I want to have a long hot shower and lie down in a comfortable bed and watch TV until I fall asleep.' He pulled a skin over his head.

'What is a war?' Zander asked Riana. She shrugged.

The flap of Zander's shelter lifted and Paul looked out. The camp was sleeping. Two Marauders sat by a fire near the cave where Correon was imprisoned. Paul crawled along the ground behind them to the entrance. It was barred by thick wooden staves. Correon was inside, sleeping fitfully. Paul quietly untied the rope securing the staves and slipped inside. He shook Correon awake and started cutting him free with his Swiss army knife.

'We're getting out of here,' he whispered as Correon came awake.

'What about my power suit?'

'I don't know where it is. Come on.'

Paul and Correon crept out of the cave and disappeared into the nearest rock passage.

Ashka and Gryvon huddled in the shelter of a rock. They had lost the Marauders' trail as the ground had turned rocky, and had been forced to spend a sleepless night in the mountains.

'Is it true that Marauders drink blood?' Gryvon asked. Ashka laughed. 'It's alright for you,' he grumbled, 'you've got a power suit.'

'If things work out,' Ashka told him,

'perhaps you can have Correon's.'

Gryvon smiled. The whinny of a horse broke the morning silence. Gryvon peered over the rock. He beckoned urgently for Ashka. A Marauder was leading Correon's horse up the mountain trail.

Cailin emerged from her tent, yawning and rubbing her arms against the morning chill. She looked around the camp and realised with a start that Correon was gone from the cave. She picked up a pot and began banging it. The alarm brought Marauders tumbling out of their shelters. 'The Spellbinder has escaped,' Cailin yelled.

The Marauders started to organise search parties. Zander ran back into his shelter and shook Riana awake. 'Correon has escaped.'

He pulled the skins off the other bed. It was empty. 'Where's Paul?'

'He must have gone with Correon.'

'They'll never find their way out of the labyrinth,' Zander said. 'When they're captured, Paul will be banished too.'

'We've got to find them first.'

'I'm not helping a Spellbinder,' Zander spat.

'Then help Paul,' Riana pleaded. 'He's not from this world.'

Zander looked at her as though she was mad. Riana pondered for a second, then took Paul's Walkman from her bag.

'Paul gave me this. It's from his world. Listen.'

She placed the headphones on Zander's head and switched the machine on. Zander's eyes widened in amazement as he heard the music from Paul's world.

A Marauder approached the entrance to the labyrinth, leading Correon's horse. He was unaware that Ashka and Gryvon were following him. A guard climbed down from the rocks and took the horse from the Marauder, who disappeared into the labyrinth. Gryvon gasped as the guard removed his hood.

'The Marauder is human!' he said to Ashka. 'He'll be no match for your power suit.'

'No! We must find the boy before he tells the Marauders how to make gunpowder.'

As the guard led the horse into some nearby trees, Ashka and Gryvon sneaked into the labyrinth.

Paul and Correon stumbled through the maze of narrow passages.

'It's no use,' Correon panted. 'We're lost.'

Paul stopped and looked around. There was no way to tell which of the passages led out of the labyrinth. He heard the sound of approaching voices. Paul pointed to a narrow crevice. 'In there.'

They squeezed into the gap just as Cailin and another Marauder appeared. Paul held his breath as they passed, then he and Correon emerged from the crevice and hurried in the opposite direction. They turned into a narrow passage but it was a dead-end.

'We're never going to get out of here,' Paul despaired.

They heard footsteps and looked desperately for a hiding place. There was nowhere to go. The walls were slippery with water and impossible to climb. They were trapped.

Desperate Measures

Paul and Correon flattened themselves against the damp rock as the footsteps got closer. Riana and Zander peered into the passage.

'You idiot,' Riana hissed, when she saw Paul. 'You've got every Marauder in the camp after you. If they catch you, they'll banish you as well as Correon.'

'Will you help us escape?' Paul asked Zander.

The Marauder boy looked curiously at Paul. 'Are you really from another world?'

'I had to tell him,' Riana said.

'Yes,' Paul admitted.

'Then I'll help you—but not the Spellbinder.'

'But I need Correon to help me get home,' Paul protested.

'What if he brings the other Spellbinders?'

'I promise you I won't,' Correon said solemnly.

There were shouts from an approaching search party. Zander stared at the Spellbinder, trying to make up his mind.

'I trust him,' Riana said.

Zander nodded. 'This way.'

Paul, Riana and Correon followed Zander through the twisting maze of passages. Paul was beginning to believe that they would get away when they emerged into a wider tunnel and came face to face with Kurn and two other Marauders. They turned to run, only to find Cailin and Tark behind them.

Kurn stared accusingly at Zander. 'Were you helping the Spellbinder to escape?'

'No!' Paul cried. 'He and Riana captured us.'

'Take the Spellbinder back to the camp,' Kurn ordered. Tark grabbed Correon.

'You've got to tell them about the gunpowder,' Riana told Paul.

'I can't!'

'Is this the secret the Spellbinders want so much?' Kurn asked.

Riana nodded.

'Bring them to the lookout.' The Marauders hustled their captives away.

Once they had gone, Ashka and Gryvon emerged from a side-passage.

'Why didn't you do something?' Gryvon asked.

'There were too many places for them to run. Patience, Gryvon.'

Ashka and Gryvon crept after Paul and the Marauders.

'Have a good day at work, Nico,' Mrs Katsonis called as Nick came out of the house, wearing his overalls and carrying his lunch.

'Thanks, Mum. See you tonight.'

Nick hurried into the garage and was surprised to see Alex and Katrina in the back seat of his car. Between them was a cardboard box containing the two-way radio equipment that Nathan had given them.

'Get out of there,' Nick growled. 'I've got to go to work.'

Alex held up the pink dismissal slip that he'd found in Nick's toolbox.

Nick stared at it in dismay. 'You haven't told Pop I lost my job?'

'No,' Alex said. 'And I won't ... if you take me and Katrina for a drive to the mountains.'

Nick's hands clenched the steering wheel in fury as he drove through the outskirts of the city. Alex and Katrina sat in the back, experimenting with the radios.

'Katrina, can you hear me?' Alex said loudly into one.

Katrina winced as his voice blared from the radio she was holding. 'You don't have to shout.'

'Sorry.' Alex put a fresh cassette in his ghettoblaster. 'Let's record some romantic mush for Nathan.'

'I can't do that stuff,' Katrina protested.

'You've got to. Nathan's expecting it for his book.'

Alex pressed the record button. 'Katrina, can you hear me ... sweetheart?' he said into his radio. His attempt to sound romantic brought a smile to Nick's face.

'Yes ... darling,' Katrina replied uncomfortably.

'I really miss you ... especially when I'm
feeding the chickens. There's one that reminds
me of you.'

Nick burst out laughing and Katrina went
red. 'She reminds you of a chicken? Katrina, if
I was you, I'd get myself a new boyfriend.'

'He's not my boyfriend!'

'So what is going on between you two?'

'We're pretending to be in love to help out a
friend,' Alex said. 'OK?'

'OK. But I think you could use a little help
from the Love Doctor.'

'Who's that?' Katrina asked.

Nick grinned. 'Me.'

Nick was driving with one hand and scribbling
on a notepad with the other. He tore off the
page and handed it to Alex.

'"Dearest Katrina,"' Alex read. '"I miss you
so much. I miss your tender kisses."'

'"I just want to rest my head against your
strong, manly chest,"' Katrina read from her

note. '"I wish we could be together forever and ever."'

Nick passed Alex another note.

'"We will be, darling heart ..."' Alex turned the note over and kept reading, '"...As soon as I've killed your parents."'

Nick cracked up and Alex angrily shut off the ghettoblaster.

'I can't do this,' Katrina wailed.

'We have to,' Alex said grumpily. 'Anyway, what's so hard about pretending to be in love with me?'

'If you love yourself so much,' Katrina snapped, 'why do you need me? You can do both voices.'

Nick started laughing again. Alex was about to hit him when Katrina pointed out of the car window. 'There's the turn-off to the camp!'

Nick swung the wheel and the car turned on to the side-road. A few minutes later it pulled up outside the deserted school camp. Alex and Katrina unloaded their equipment and hurried up the trail that led to the cave.

A hot, dry wind sucked the moisture from Paul's eyes as he stood with Correon and Kurn on the ridge which surrounded the Marauder camp. Far below them, a desolate landscape stretched to the horizon. Paul realised he was looking at the devastation the ancient Spellbinders had wreaked in their quest for power. He wondered if the rest of the world looked like this.

'The Wastelands, Paul,' Kurn said solemnly, 'the place of banishment. The Spellbinders left me out there, without water or food. That is where we will take Correon: unless you tell us about the gunpowder.'

Correon fixed Paul with a steely gaze. 'You must not.'

'But you'll die!'

Correon reached into his cloak and took out the old journal. He offered it to Kurn. 'This was written by an old Spellbinder. It proves that the Darkness was caused by the Spellbinders.'

Kurn leafed quickly through the pages.

'Their hunger for knowledge almost destroyed the whole world,' Correon explained. 'That's why you must let the boy go. His knowledge is too dangerous.'

'We might believe you,' Kurn said sarcastically, 'if any of us could read.' He threw the book to the ground and turned to Paul. 'This is your last chance.'

'Let me tell them,' Paul begged Correon.

'No! Just find a way to get that journal to the Regents.'

Paul nodded. He picked up the journal and put it in his pocket. Correon smiled at him gratefully.

'The Spellbinder will be taken to the Wastelands,' Kurn ordered.

The Marauders gathered as Tark shoved Correon back into the camp.

'We weren't wearing fine clothes when we were banished,' Tark yelled.

Paul and Riana watched helplessly as Tark yanked off Correon's cloak and threw it on the fire. The Marauders cheered as it burst into flames.

Ashka and Gryvon crouched in a passage, watching. 'Let's get Paul now,' Gryvon whispered.

'No. There are too many. I wish I had some help.'

Gryvon looked back at the camp, feeling useless. Then his eyes lit up. 'Ashka, look.' He pointed to Correon's power suit hanging inside Kurn's tent.

'Can you get it?' Ashka asked.

While the Marauders watched the cloak burn, Gryvon crawled around the perimeter of the camp to the tent. He took down the power suit and crept back to Ashka. She took a spare powerstone from the bag Gryvon had rescued from the crashed flying ship.

'Listen carefully,' she told Gryvon as she fitted the powerstone to the suit. 'This is what we're going to do.'

Katrina and Alex were perched among the rocks above the cave, using a map and a compass to align their radio antenna in the direction of Alex's garage.

'Are you sure this rig is going to be powerful enough?' Katrina asked.

'Nathan promised me that it would transmit back to the city,' Alex replied, uncoiling a cable connected to the antenna. 'Once we put this radio into the cave, anything the Spellbinders broadcast will be relayed to the other radio at home.'

Katrina picked up the solar cell and started to climb up the rocks. Alex scrambled down to the cave, laying out the cable as he went.

While he was waiting for Katrina, Alex put a tape in his ghettoblaster. Rap music blared from the speakers, echoing around the hillside. Alex started moving to the beat.

'Can't you turn that up any more?' Katrina yelled as she joined him. 'There are some people in Antarctica who can't hear it.'

Alex turned the tape off. Katrina plugged the cable into one of the two-way radios and turned it on. They were both disappointed to hear only static coming from the speaker.

'Make sure it's tuned to the right frequency,' Alex said.

'I have,' Katrina snapped.

'You don't have to bite my head off.'

'Sorry. I'm just worried about Paul.'

The radio crackled, then Ashka's voice came from it: 'Gryvon, are you ready?'

'Yes, Ashka,' Gryvon replied.

Katrina and Alex stared at each other with excitement. 'Ashka's the Spellbinder we spoke to,' Katrina said.

'Wait for my signal,' Ashka continued. 'Paul must not escape.'

The radio went silent.

'Paul's in danger,' Katrina said anxiously. 'We've got to warn him.'

Alex put his ghettoblaster in front of the radio and reached for the play button. 'This should get his attention.'

Hidden at the entrance to a passage, Ashka watched as Kurn and Tark pushed Correon past the silent Marauders. The old Spellbinder's hands were tied behind his back but he faced his fate bravely. Paul and Riana stood together, watching helplessly as Correon was taken to the Wastelands.

Suddenly rap music blasted from Ashka's

Eyestone. The Marauders looked round in stunned surprise as the strange music echoed around their camp.

'I know that music,' Riana exclaimed. 'It's "Chocolate Rapper". What's going on?'

Before Paul could answer, the music was replaced by Katrina's voice. 'Paul, if you can hear me, this is Katrina. Some Spellbinder called Ashka is trying to capture you. Run!'

'Ashka must have followed us,' Paul yelled to Kurn. 'Get your people out of here.'

'Spellbinders!' Kurn shouted. 'Into the labyrinth!'

Ashka realised her chance to capture Paul was slipping away. She stepped out of the passage and strode into the camp. 'Give me the boy!' she yelled.

The sight of a Spellbinder threw the Marauders into a panic. They dropped their possessions and ran for the safety of the labyrinth.

Kurn and Zander left Correon and charged at Ashka, hurling rocks. She energised her power suit and launched a power-bolt. Kurn and Zander hit the ground as the bolt seared over their heads and struck a tent, which burst into flames. The fire spread from tent to tent, and the camp began to burn.

Paul ran to Correon and untied his hands. He pulled the Spellbinder towards the other end of the camp, away from Ashka.

Unable to stop the music blaring from his Eyestone, Gryvon threw it under a rock. He looked up and saw Paul and Correon running his way. Gryvon energised his power suit and stepped out of in front of them. 'Ashka, I've got him!' Gryvon bellowed. He fired a bolt.

Paul threw Correon to the ground and the bolt whistled over their heads, bringing down another shelter.

'You can't get away, Paul,' Gryvon gloated, preparing to hurl another bolt.

'Gryvon!' Riana called.

Gryvon looked up and saw Riana standing above him on the windmill beside the water tank. She pushed the aqueduct out and a torrent of water cascaded down on the Apprentice, knocking him to the ground. Sparks flew as the powerstone in his suit shorted out. Paul helped Correon to his feet.

'Paul! Look out!' Zander shouted from across the camp.

Paul turned and saw Ashka running towards them.

'You're the one she wants. Run!' Correon pushed Paul into the labyrinth and blocked Ashka's path. She shoved him aside and went after Paul.

Gryvon got to his feet, dripping wet. He realised that Marauders were heading his way and tried to energise his power suit. Nothing happened. Gryvon beat a hasty retreat into the labyrinth.

Paul raced along a passage, only to find it was another dead-end. He turned to go back but found himself facing Ashka.

'Alright, I give up. You've got me.'

Paul slumped to the ground. But as Ashka approached, he rolled through a narrow crack under a rock, escaping into a passage on the other side. Ashka screamed in frustration.

In another passage, a dripping Gryvon fitted a fresh powerstone to his suit. He looked up in surprise as Cailin and Rinske ran into the passage. Gryvon raised his arms to energise his power suit.

'Leave these people alone. They have done you no harm.'

Gryvon whirled around and saw Correon behind him.

'They are enemies of the Spellbinders,' Gryvon said.

Anger blazed in Correon's eyes. 'I am a Regent,' he roared, 'you must obey me.'

Gryvon remembered that Correon had disobeyed the other Regents and helped the boy to escape. If he captured Correon, the Regents might make him a Spellbinder. He energised the power suit.

Correon stepped between Gryvon and Cailin. 'You are an Apprentice. You have no right to wear a power suit. Take it off!'

Gryvon stared defiantly at Correon. There was a blur of movement in the air as Riana leaped down from the rocks and kicked Gryvon in the back. He sprawled on the ground and Correon leaped onto him, pulling the powerstone from the suit. He hauled Gryvon to his feet. Gryvon kicked Correon in the shin, broke free and raced out of the passage.

'You help these people,' Correon said to Riana. 'I'm going to try and stop Ashka.' He ran back towards the camp.

Paul ran between the rocks, looking desperately for a way out of the endless maze of passages. He raced around a corner and collided with Gryvon. They both sprawled to the ground. Paul struggled to his feet but Gryvon held onto his leg.

'I've got him, Ashka!'

Ashka ran into the passage and saw Gryvon struggling with Paul. She grabbed him. Gryvon got to his feet, grinning triumphantly. They looked around at the sound of Correon's voice. 'Ashka!'

Ashka clamped her hand over Paul's mouth and pulled him out of sight. Gryvon huddled with them.

'Ashka!' Correon called again as he came into view.

Kurn and Tark leaped out of a side-passage and grabbed him.

'So you are working with the other

pellbinder,' Kurn snarled.

'No! I'm trying to stop her. Let me go.' Correon struggled but the burly Marauders dragged him away.

'You have to help him,' Paul pleaded to Ashka. 'They're going to take him to the Wastelands.'

'Good,' Ashka replied. 'Gryvon, let's find a way out of this place. We'll come back later and destroy these Marauders.'

'The Marauders aren't a threat,' Paul said desperately. 'They didn't cause the Darkness. It was the old Spellbinders.'

'Impossible!' Ashka said.

'I can prove it.' Paul took the old Spellbinder journal from his pocket and gave it to her.

'It's true,' Gryvon said as Ashka turned the ancient pages. 'I heard Correon read it.'

'That's why Correon wants to send me back to my world,' Paul explained. 'He's worried the same thing will happen again. You have to show this to the Regents.'

Ashka hurled the journal to the ground and energised her power suit. Paul watched in dismay as she fired a bolt at the book. The old, dry pages of the precious journal burst into flames.

A rock clattered to the ground in front of them and Ashka and Gryvon looked up. Zander was clinging to the rock face, one leg dangling where he had lost his footing. Gryvon leaped up and grabbed Zander's leg, pulling him down. He hit the ground with a thud and the Walkman fell from his clothes. Gryvon picked it up. Ashka hauled Zander to his feet.

'If you value your life,' she snarled, 'show us the way out of here.'

Zander's head poked out of the entrance to the labyrinth. There was nobody in sight. Ashka pushed him out of the passage and Gryvon pulled Paul after them. Ashka opened her Eyestone and spoke into it. 'Regents, this is Ashka. The Marauders have killed Correon.'

There was a crackle of static, then Lukan's voice came from the Eyestone: 'Where are you? We'll send a flying ship.'

As Ashka gave instructions to Lukan,

Gryvon put on the headphones and fiddled with the controls of the Walkman.

'How do you make this work?' he asked Paul.

Paul saw his chance. 'I'll show you.' He turned the volume control right up and then pressed the play button. Rap music boomed through Gryvon's head and he howled in pain. Paul shoved him into Ashka. 'Run!' he yelled to Zander.

As they raced back towards the labyrinth, Gryvon tackled Paul and brought him down. Zander made it to the entrance and disappeared back into the labyrinth.

Kurn and the Marauders were gathered in a thick grove of trees outside the labyrinth. Correon sat on the ground, his hands bound once more.

'You can't banish him,' Riana protested. 'He risked his life for your family.'

'A vote was taken,' Kurn said stubbornly.

'Then I change my vote,' Cailin said.

'We can't just let him go,' Kurn said, exasperated by his wife's attitude. 'He led the

Spellbinders to our camp.'

'Kurn!'

Everyone looked round as Zander raced into the trees. 'Ashka's got Paul,' he panted. 'A flying ship's coming.'

'If the Spellbinders force Paul to give them gunpowder,' Correon said, struggling to his feet, 'they'll wipe out every one of you. Let me go to the Regents. I can bring peace between the Spellbinders and the Marauders.'

'Why should we listen to you?' Tark asked.

'Because he's been telling the truth,' Zander said. 'It was the Spellbinders who caused the Darkness. I heard the Apprentice say so.'

The Marauders stared at Correon, stunned by the news.

'You have to let Correon go,' Riana said. 'He's your only chance.'

The flying ship came to rest in the castle courtyard, and Ashka and Gryvon dragged Paul out of the hatch. He was gagged and his hands were tied. Paul was certain now that he would never get home.

'Ashka,' Lukan called as they headed into the gardens.

Gryvon pulled Paul behind some shrubs as Lukan and Marna came out of the castle. Ashka bowed to the Regents.

'Correon is dead?' Marna asked sadly.

'The Marauders threw him off a cliff,' Ashka replied gravely. 'I couldn't do anything to stop them. If we do not wipe these Marauders out, they will bring the Darkness again.'

'Do whatever is necessary,' Lukan said.

Ashka bowed as Lukan and Marna went back into the castle. Once they were gone, Gryvon and Ashka dragged Paul down the steps leading to the cellar under the castle. Ashka unbolted the door and Gryvon pushed Paul inside. Paul despairingly surveyed the dismal surroundings. He was right back where he had started. Gryvon removed his gag.

'Paul, you could earn my gratitude by helping me destroy the Marauders,' Ashka said persuasively.

'They're people,' Paul protested.

'Only you and I and Gryvon know that.'

'I'm not telling,' Gryvon said, smirking.

265

'You can't keep it a secret forever,' Paul said. 'When the Regents discover the truth ...'

'It will be too late. Give me the secret of the gunpowder or Gryvon will nail up the door. No-one will ever find you.'

Paul knew that Ashka meant what she said. 'Alright. Alright. I'll make you some gunpowder.'

But as Ashka smiled victoriously, a plan was forming in Paul's mind.

Riana was helping Zander pack up his tent while the other Marauders salvaged what they could from their burnt-out camp. Riana looked up in surprise as Katrina's voice came from the labyrinth: 'Hello? Can anyone hear me?'

The voice continued as Riana and Zander ran into the labyrinth, searching for its source.

'My name is Katrina.'

'And I'm Alex,' another voice said.

'Here,' Zander yelled.

Riana turned to see Zander retrieving the Eyestone that Gryvon had thrown away.

'We're from the world next door to yours,' Katrina continued, 'if that makes any sense.

We're friends of a boy called Paul Reynolds. Tell him we can help him get home.'

Riana took the Eyestone from Zander. 'I can hear you,' she yelled into it. 'I know where Paul is.'

'Talk to me!' Katrina's voice called from the Eyestone.

'I am,' Riana yelled back.

'Is anyone there?' Katrina asked desperately.

Riana stared at the Eyestone. 'What's wrong with it?'

'Maybe the Eyestone needs a power suit to make them hear you,' Zander suggested.

'Answer me,' Katrina yelled into the radio. She paced around Alex's garage, her frustration building. Paul could have been captured and thrown into a dungeon. Or worse.

'Leave it,' Alex said gently, taking the radio from her. 'No-one's going to answer. You go home. I'll stay up and keep listening. If I hear anything, I'll tape it. Then we can play it to Paul's father and he'll help us. OK?'

'OK. Thanks, Alex.'

'We'll get Paul back. I promise.'

Katrina kissed Alex on the cheek, then hurried out before he could say anything. Alex was surprised, not only by the fact that Katrina had kissed him but that he had liked it.

Riana and Zander watched Kurn examining the Eyestone.

'We have always wanted to capture one of these,' he said excitedly. 'Now we can hear what the Spellbinders are planning.'

'But Paul's friends are trying to talk to him,' Riana protested. 'I have to take it to the castle.'

'No. The Eyestone must remain with us.'

Kurn walked away, taking the Eyestone with him.

Without a second thought, Riana headed towards the labyrinth.

Zander hurried after her. 'Where are you going?'

'I've got to take the message to Paul.' She disappeared into a passage.

In the gloomy cellar, Paul poured iron filings into a pot that was heating over a fire. Ashka and Gryvon watched every move he made, alert for trickery. 'Gunpowder is really very simple to make,' Paul said. 'First you heat some metal filings. Then stir in some sulphur ... goodyellow. Gryvon, would you start stirring?'

Gryvon stirred the pot with a wooden spoon. Behind him, Paul dipped a wad of cloth into a jug of water.

'What are the cloth and the water for?' Ashka asked.

'So I can strain the final mixture. How's it looking Gryvon?'

Gryvon peered into the pot. 'It doesn't look like gunpowder yet.'

'Ashka, would you add just a touch more goodyellow?'

Ashka added more sulphur to the pot.

'How does it look now?' Paul asked, backing away from the fire.

A thick yellow gas suddenly rose from the pot as the chemical reaction took place. Ashka and Gryvon were engulfed in clouds of foul-smelling rotten egg gas. They started gagging.

Paul held the wet cloth over his nose and mouth to filter out the fumes. While Ashka and Gryvon choked and coughed, Paul lifted the pot from the fire. He raced out of the door and up the steps into the garden, fumes from the pot billowing behind him.

Ashka staggered up the steps, tears streaming from her eyes. 'Stop him!' she wheezed.

Guards appeared and Paul hurled the pot to the ground in front of them. It shattered, enveloping the guards in gas. They began retching. Paul ran past them and into the castle.

'You idiot!' Correon yelled at the sentries outside the castle gate. He was dirty and saddle-sore from his ride from the Marauders' camp and was in no mood for arguments. 'Of course I'm a Spellbinder. I'm Correon.'

Borin's eyes narrowed suspiciously. 'Correon's dead. The Marauders killed him.'

'That's his horse,' Mort said. 'How did you get it?'

The sentries started to drag Correon off the horse. But as they struggled, the castle gates burst open, and guards and Apprentices rushed out, retching from the rotten egg gas. Correon broke free of the guards and galloped through the gate.

Lukan and Marna looked up in surprise as the doors to the Regents' chamber crashed open and Paul raced in.

'Ashka was lying,' he panted. 'The Marauders aren't monsters. They're people. She didn't see them throw Correon off a cliff ...'

Ashka and Gryvon staggered in behind him, tears streaming from their eyes.

'The boy has poisoned the castle,' Ashka gasped. 'I will deal with him.' She seized Paul, but then realised the Regents were staring in amazement at something behind her. She turned to look. Correon was standing in the doorway.

The Centre of Power

Paul broke free from Gryvon and ran across the Regents' chamber to Correon. 'I thought you'd gone to the Wastelands,' he exclaimed, overjoyed to see the old Spellbinder alive.

'We were told the Marauders had killed you,' Marna said looking at Ashka suspiciously.

'It must have been someone else,' Ashka spluttered then forced a smile. 'Welcome home, Regent. I'm pleased to see you're alive.'

'I doubt it,' Correon snapped. 'What other lies have you been telling?'

Ashka shot Correon a blistering look but said nothing.

'Did you show the Regents the journal?' Correon asked Paul.

'No. Ashka burnt it.'

'What journal?' Lukan asked.

'An old Spellbinder wrote it,' Correon replied. 'The Marauders didn't cause the Darkness. It was the ...'

'Stop,' Ashka cried. 'You have called me a liar in front of the Council. I challenge you!'

Marna gasped. 'Ashka, no-one has invoked that law for years.'

'Correon has called me a liar,' Ashka repeated. 'Spellbinder law gives me the right to challenge him.'

'It's more important that we find the truth here,' Marna protested.

'Correon has dishonoured me,' Ashka insisted.

Lukan nodded gravely. 'The law is the law. Correon, a challenge has been issued. It must be answered.'

Correon bowed to Ashka. 'I accept.'

'The challenge will be decided tomorrow morning,' Lukan announced.

'I want my power suit,' Correon snapped at Gryvon. 'Bring it to my apartment.'

'And I want this,' Paul said. He snatched his Walkman from Gryvon's belt and followed Correon out.

'So how do you fight this challenge?' Paul asked as he watched Correon draw a chalk circle on the floor of his apartment. 'With swords?'

'With power suits. Each Spellbinder stands inside a circle like this. If you fall from the circle, you lose.'

'So you won't be hurt?'

'I hope not.' Correon strapped a metal shield to his right forearm. 'Will you help me practise?' He handed Paul a basket of apples.

'What do I do with these?'

'Throw them at me. I'll try to avoid them.'

Paul shrugged and threw an apple. It hit Correon who lost his balance and fell out of the circle.

'I wasn't ready,' Correon complained. He stepped back into the circle and began ducking and weaving. Paul threw another apple. Correon dodged it easily and smiled.

'How many challenges have you fought?' Paul asked.

'Well, none actually. But I've seen one, a long time ago. Come on!'

Trying to hide his dismay, Paul threw

another apple. Correon deflected it with his shield. 'Again!'

Paul hurled another apple. Correon caught it and flung it back. Paul cried out as it hit him. 'What happens if you lose?' he asked, rubbing his arm.

'I won't lose.'

'What happens?'

'I will cease to be a Spellbinder.'

'Take back the challenge,' Paul pleaded. 'Apologise to Ashka.'

'It's too late to apologise,' Correon said. 'I wouldn't want to anyway. Again.'

Paul threw two apples at once.

Gryvon was spying through the keyhole of Correon's door. He saw Correon deflect one apple and deftly catch the other. 'See?' he heard Correon gloat. 'Ashka doesn't stand a chance.'

Gryvon hurried back to Ashka's room where he found her practising defensive moves in front of the mirror.

'What will happen if Correon wins tomorrow?' Gryvon asked her.

'In that unlikely event, you can forget about

ever becoming a Spellbinder.'

Gryvon realised he had better make sure that Ashka won. His future depended on it.

The next morning, Correon and Paul returned to the apartment after an early breakfast. Paul helped the old Spellbinder into his power suit. Paul had stayed up late the previous evening, polishing the copper fittings on the suit to a gleaming finish. 'In a suit like this,' Correon said proudly, 'I can't lose.'

'You look great,' Paul said, filming him with the video-camera. 'The people back in my world are going to be very impressed.' He turned off the camera. 'Let's go. I'm looking forward to getting Ashka's defeat on tape.'

'I'm sorry,' Correon said, 'only Spellbinders and their Apprentices are permitted to view the challenge.'

Paul was disappointed but managed a smile. 'I'll see you back here after you've won.'

'And then we'll find a way to get you home,' Correon promised.

Paul followed him into the corridor. 'Good luck,' he called as the Spellbinder strode jauntily away. Gryvon was watching them. Paul noticed that there was a bandage around the Apprentice's hand. Gryvon gave Paul a sly smile and walked off.

As Paul came back into Correon's apartment, he saw something glittering on the floor. He knelt and saw tiny shavings of copper under the hook where Correon's power suit had been hanging. Half-hidden under a pile of books was a broken piece of saw blade. Paul went cold as he realised someone had been tampering with the power suit. Then he noticed a drop of blood on the floor and remembered Gryvon's bandaged hand.

Correon and Ashka stood facing each other inside circles of white sand at either end of the Regents' chamber. Lukan and Marna watched from the balcony above. Gathered around them were the other sixteen Spellbinders and their Apprentices.

'Will neither of you reconsider this?' Marna asked.

Correon and Ashka remained stubbornly silent.

Lukan raised his hand. 'The loser is the first to leave their circle.'

Correon and Ashka struck their wrists together, energising their power suits. Lukan dropped his hand and the challenge began.

Ashka hurled a bolt of energy. Correon twisted, and deflected it with his shield. He smiled at Ashka. She would have to do better than that.

Paul raced up the corridor to the door of the Regents' chamber but two guards blocked his way. 'A challenge is in progress,' one said sternly. 'No-one may enter.'

'But Regent Correon's suit has been sabotaged.'

'No-one may enter,' the guard repeated.

Paul turned and raced desperately back down the corridor.

In the Regents' chamber, Correon hurled a power-bolt at Ashka. She dodged it but Correon quickly threw another. Sparks flew as the bolt hit Ashka and she staggered, nearly falling from the circle. Correon was about to

278

throw another bolt when sparks suddenly erupted from the right shoulder of his power suit. Power faded from that arm. In the balcony, Gryvon smirked. Ashka regained her balance and turned to face Correon. Power crackled around her fingers as she prepared to hurl another bolt.

'Help me! Somebody help me!'

The guards outside the Regents' chamber looked up at the sound of Paul's voice. One hurried up the corridor and looked around the corner. He beckoned for the other guard to join him. A small wooden chest lay on the floor. Paul's voice was coming from inside it: 'Somebody help me. I'm stuck in here and I can't get out. Help!'

The guards stared nervously at the box. 'Go on,' one said. 'Whatever's in there can't be very big.'

The other guard warily opened the chest. The video-camera was inside and Paul's face was on the tiny screen. 'Let me out,' he cried.

'How did you get in there?' the guard asked.

As they stared in bewilderment at the

screen, a door opened behind them and Paul sneaked out. He ran towards the Regents' chamber.

Correon dodged another bolt from Ashka. He was tiring but not beaten. He raised his left arm to retaliate but another copper cable snapped. As Correon desperately tried to reconnect the sparking ends of the cable, Ashka fired a bolt. It scored a direct hit on the belt of Correon's power suit. One of the powerstones burned out in a massive shower of sparks. The discharge hurled Correon out of the circle and he landed heavily on the floor.

'Now admit you are the one who is lying,' Ashka demanded.

'You know I was not,' Correon croaked.

The Spellbinders in the balcony were silent as Ashka raised her arm to hurl a final bolt at the defenceless Correon. The doors burst open and Paul ran into the chamber.

'Ashka! I'll give you the gunpowder,' he yelled. 'Just don't hurt Correon.'

Ashka lowered her arm and the power faded from her suit. Paul ran to the dazed Spellbinder and knelt beside him. 'Are you alright?'

'Yes,' Correon groaned. 'But I lost. I'm sorry.'

'Regents,' Ashka called to the balcony. 'I demand the winner's right.'

'But Gryvon sabotaged ...' Paul began.

'Silence,' Ashka snapped.

Lukan got reluctantly to his feet. 'Correon, you are no longer a Spellbinder. You will be banished immediately. Remove your power suit.'

Paul saw the triumphant smile on Ashka's face and his heart sank. Now he would never get home.

Gryvon pushed Paul into the castle courtyard. Lukan, Marna and Ashka were waiting near a flying ship. Two guards led Correon out of the castle. The Spellbinder looked old and frail.

'I'm sorry, Correon,' Marna said. 'The Spellbinders will be poorer without you.'

Correon smiled his thanks.

'Take him to the ship,' Lukan ordered.

Ashka climbed into the flying ship and the guards pushed Correon towards it. Paul broke away from Gryvon and threw his arms around Correon.

'You opened my eyes to the world, Paul,' Correon said, his voice full of feeling. 'I hope you find a way to return to yours.'

Paul took out his Walkman and slipped it into Correon's hand. 'Take this,' he whispered. 'As long as the batteries last, you'll be able to hear the Spellbinders.'

Tears welled in Correon's eyes.

'Goodbye, Spellbinder,' Paul said bravely.

'Goodbye, Apprentice.'

The guards forced Correon up the ladder and into the ship. The hatch clanged shut and the throbbing sound began. With a shower of sparks, the ship rose into the air.

'You have no friends left now,' Gryvon said to Paul.

Riana hurried between the trees towards the castle. She had run nearly all the way from the Marauders' camp and was exhausted. She looked up as a flying ship appeared over the castle walls and flew away. Suddenly an arm reached out from behind a tree and grabbed her. It was Mort, the sentry. Riana struggled in his grip as he dragged her towards the guard hut beside the castle gate.

'It's that girl who broke into the castle,' Mort yelled. 'Ashka offered a reward for her.'

Borin hurried out of the hut.

'Let me go,' Riana protested. 'I'm a friend of the Regent Correon.'

'Correon's not a Regent any more,' Borin said. 'He's not even a Spellbinder. That was him in the flying ship: Ashka's taking him to the Wastelands.'

Riana was horrified. Without Correon, Paul was at Ashka's mercy.

'Call the castle guard,' Mort told Borin.

'No! If we give the girl to them, they'll take the reward.'

'We'll tie her up here until Ashka returns,' Mort decided. 'Throw me the rope.'

Borin lifted a coil of rope from a hook on the side of the guard house and threw it. As Mort went to catch it, Riana pushed him. The rope hit Mort in the head and Riana broke free. Borin tried to grab her but Riana dodged around him and raced into the guard hut. She slammed the door behind her.

'You idiot,' Mort screamed at Borin.

'You told me to throw it.'

They stared at the bolted door. 'The last time she went in there,' Mort remembered, 'she escaped out the window.' They raced around the back of the guardhouse to intercept her.

Riana opened the front door, scooped up the coil of rope and ran towards the trees. Bellowing with rage, Borin and Mort went after her.

Riana scrambled up a tree trunk and hid in the foliage as the sentries searched below. As they moved deeper into the forest, Riana jumped down from the tree and hurried to the castle wall. She tied her bolas to the end of the rope, whirled them and flung them high into the air. The bolas wrapped around the battlements at the top of the wall. Riana pulled the rope taut and began to climb it, hand over hand.

Riana clambered over the battlements and onto the castle roof. She looked anxiously around but no-one had seen her. She ran to a door at the base of a tower and went inside.

Riana sneaked down through the castle to the cells. There was no sign of Paul. She decided to look in the cellar where he had made the fireworks and made her way towards a staircase. She was about to descend when she heard footsteps coming from above. She threw herself back around the corner and out of sight.

Gryvon appeared, escorting a frightened-looking Paul down the staircase. Riana was about to tackle Gryvon when she realised that he was wearing a power suit beneath his cloak. She carefully followed them down the stairs.

Gryvon pushed Paul towards Correon's apartment. The old Spellbinder's precious books sat in untidy piles in the corridor outside. Gryvon shoved Paul through the door.

The untidy apartment had been cleaned and Correon's possessions replaced with Ashka's. Ashka was hanging up her power suit. 'Welcome, Paul,' she said, smiling. 'What do you think of my new accommodation? More

285

fitting for a Regent, I think.' She sat in Correon's chair.

'You're not a Regent yet,' Paul reminded her.

'I will be,' Ashka gloated, 'once you give me the secret of the gunpowder. And I warn you, my patience is at an end. Sit down.'

As Paul sat, he saw his video-camera on the desk and realised that Ashka must have retrieved it from the guards. A desperate plan formed in his head. He looked towards the door. 'Morning, Lukan,' he said cheerily.

Ashka and Gryvon whirled around. Paul quickly switched the camera to record and pointed it at Ashka. She turned angrily back to him. 'I'm in no mood for games.'

'I didn't think the Regents were in on your plans,' Paul said.

'The Regents are fools,' Ashka told him. 'They have let the people lose respect for the Spellbinders. Paul, you have no choice in this. Tell me how to make gunpowder.'

'You want the gunpowder to use against the Regents,' Paul said. 'You want to rule the Spellbinders.'

'Very perceptive. And when I do, I can make

your life here very pleasant. Or very un-pleasant.'

Gryvon noticed Paul swivelling the camera to track Ashka as she paced. He moved behind Paul and saw Ashka's image on the screen.

'Ashka, he's using the picture box,' he yelled. 'He is capturing you and your words.'

Before Ashka could grab the camera, the door opened and Riana staggered in, her face hidden behind a tall pile of Correon's books.

'I don't want them in here,' Ashka snapped. 'Get out!'

'There's no need to be rude,' Riana replied, and threw the heavy books at Ashka, knocking her over.

'Riana,' Gryvon cried in amazement.

He pulled back his cloak and energised Correon's power suit. Riana backed away fearfully. Paul fell to his knees.

'No, Gryvon,' he pleaded. 'Please.'

Gryvon hesitated, enjoying his moment of power. Paul yanked the rug from under his feet and Gryvon sprawled on top of Ashka.

'That felt good,' Paul said, grinning.

'Come on,' Riana yelled and raced out.

Paul grabbed the camera and followed her.

'Ashka will call the guard,' Riana panted as they fled along the corridor.

'Not while I've got this.' Paul held up the camera. 'She won't want the Regents to hear what's on it.'

Riana ran up a staircase.

'Riana, we should be going down.'

'I know what I'm doing.'

'We'll be trapped up there!'

'Will you shut up! I've got a rope on the wall.'

'Why didn't you say so?'

Riana burst through the door at the top of the stairs. Across the roof a guard was suspiciously examining Riana's rope. He looked up and saw Paul and Riana.

'Want to try my plan?' Paul asked.

He and Riana raced back down the stairs.

'What is your plan?' Riana asked.

'I don't have one,' Paul admitted. 'I'm sorry. You shouldn't have come after me.'

'I had to. I've got a message from your friend Katrina.'

'What?!'

'I heard her on the Eyestone. She can help you get home.'

They raced into a corridor and saw Gryvon running towards them. Paul and Riana ran back to the staircase and fled down it. The staircase led to a deserted tunnel deep in the bowels of the castle. The air was filled with a loud throbbing.

The tunnel opened up into a cavernous chamber. A huge metal cage had been constructed around the perimeter. In the centre of the cage was an enormous arch of gleaming powerstone. Tremendous bolts of power crackled between the top of the arch and a metal plate suspended above it.

'That's a huge electro-magnetic generator,' Paul said excitedly. Riana followed as Paul crept through the doorway into the cage. 'This must be where their energy comes from. It's the power centre for the whole castle.'

They heard the creak of wheels in the tunnel and hid as two Apprentices rolled a trolley of dull powerstones into the cage. Paul watched curiously as they positioned it under the arch. Power crackled around the trolley and the powerstones began to gleam.

'See?' Paul whispered. 'That's how they recharge old powerstones.'

Ashka and Gryvon ran into the chamber. 'Everyone leave,' Ashka shouted.

The Apprentices left their task and hurried towards the tunnel.

'Guard the entrance,' she told Gryvon. 'Don't let anyone in.'

Gryvon followed the Apprentices out. Ashka strode to the centre of the chamber. 'I know you're in here, Paul,' she shouted. 'Give yourself up or the girl will suffer.'

Paul looked at Riana. She shook her head and they moved deeper into the shadows. Paul tripped over a long iron bar and froze, but Ashka turned towards the sound. 'Come out, Paul.'

Paul's mind raced as he tried to think of a way out of their predicament. He looked at the iron bar then at the arch and an idea started to form. He handed Riana the video-camera and picked up the bar.

'What are you going to do?' Riana whispered.

'Blow a few fuses, I hope.'

Before Riana could ask what he meant, Paul stepped from hiding.

'Where's the girl and the picture box?' Ashka demanded.

Paul didn't answer. He raised the bar and Ashka laughed.

'Don't be a fool. You can't hurt me with that.'

Paul turned and tossed the iron bar at the arch. As it struck, the bar bridged both legs of the arch and caused a massive short circuit. The whole chamber lit up as energy blazed around the cage. Ashka's power suit was attracted by the powerful magnetic field of the arch. Struggling vainly, she was dragged across the chamber. She stuck to the arch like a fly in a magnetic web, her body jerking as power crackled around her. 'Gryvon,' she shouted, 'help me.'

Gryvon and the Apprentices ran into the chamber. Gryvon saw Ashka dangling help-lessly from the arch and went towards her.

'No,' Ashka cried. 'Take off your power suit.'

Gryvon pulled off his suit and ran to Ashka's aid. He picked up a long wooden pole and started to pry her off the arch. Behind, Paul and Riana hurried towards the doorway to the cage. Paul picked up Gryvon's power suit as they raced into the tunnel.

In the castle courtyard, Spellbinders, Apprentices and guards were running in panic as massive bolts of power shot from the tower on the roof. Paul and Riana crept out of the castle and saw that the gate was unguarded. As they raced towards it, the discharge from the tower returned to normal. Paul and Riana dived under a flying ship as the guards went back to the gate.

'Now what?' Riana asked.

Paul looked at the power suit he was holding. 'I've got another idea.' He crawled through the hatch of the flying ship.

Riana followed him inside. 'What are you doing?'

'Help me get the suit on.'

Riana helped Paul into the heavy power

suit. It was too large for him and he looked ridiculous as he sat in the control seat.

'Do you know what you're doing?' Riana asked anxiously.

'I've watched Ashka fly this thing. It looks pretty simple.' He pulled one of the levers. Nothing happened.

Riana glanced out of the window and saw Ashka and Gryvon run into the courtyard. 'Ashka's coming,' Riana yelled. 'If you don't hurry up you can ask her!'

Paul struck his wrists together as he'd seen the Spellbinders do. Sparks flew and the suit energised. The controls came alive and a glow appeared in the ship's powerstone. It began to throb with power.

In the courtyard, Ashka looked up as she heard the sound. 'They're in the ship!'

She and Gryvon raced towards the flying ship. Riana saw them coming.

'Hurry up, Paul.'

'Hang on.'

Paul pulled back on the controls and the nose of the ship started to lift.

'I'm doing it!' Paul crowed.

The ship fell back on the tower with a crash. Paul yanked on the control lever and the ship rose but then crashed back again.

'I can't get it to lift off,' Paul wailed as the ship lurched up and down. 'We're stuck!'

Spellbinder Jack

Riana clung to the back of the control seat as the flying ship lurched violently up and down.

'Why aren't we moving?' she yelled.

'I don't know! Something's holding us down.' Paul yanked on the controls. The ship lurched again but still wouldn't take off.

'The ship's powered by magnets: maybe I have to reverse the polarity of its powerstone.' Paul desperately examined the ship's controls.

Through the window in the nose, Riana saw Ashka energise her power suit. 'You better do it quickly!' she cried.

Paul noticed that a heavy lever beside the control seat was connected to the gleaming powerstone in the floor of the ship. He pulled the lever and the powerstone began to rotate. The ship slowly started to rise. 'I did it,' Paul yelled triumphantly.

The flying ship lurched as Ashka's power-bolt struck it. Paul struggled to keep the ship from crashing as energy crackled around its interior. He was insulated by the control seat but the electrical discharge threw Riana to the floor.

Outside, Ashka and Gryvon watched as the ship flew unsteadily towards the castle walls. Ashka hurled a second bolt. The ship lurched again but cleared the wall by a hair's breadth and swooped away.

'Find out where the nearest flying ship is and call it back to the castle,' Ashka screamed at Gryvon.

Riana opened her eyes and looked at Paul, who was concentrating on the ship's controls. 'What happened?' she asked.

She got unsteadily to her feet and looked out of the nose of the flying ship. The ground was far below them. 'We're flying!' she screamed.

'What did you expect?' Paul said calmly. 'This is a flying ship. Which way to Clayhill?'

Riana took a moment to get her bearings

from the unfamiliar viewpoint and then pointed east.

'Bron and Maran are going to be very impressed when I bring you home in this,' Paul chuckled. He carefully moved the controls and the cumbersome flying ship turned towards Clayhill.

Mr Kennett was writing a series of maths equations on the blackboard while Katrina and the rest of the class copied them down. Alex was dozing at his desk, exhausted by his sleepless night listening for Paul. He snapped awake as Gryvon's voice blared from the two-way radio in the bag under Katrina's desk. 'All flying ships, report your positions.'

Mr Kennett spun around and looked suspiciously at the class. He could see nothing amiss and went back to writing.

Katrina reached under her desk. As she opened her bag, the radio crackled again. 'This is Gallia. I'm at ...' Katrina switched off the radio.

'Who is doing that?' Mr Kennett bellowed, whirling around.

Alex leaped to his feet. 'Me, sir. I was having a dream.'

'And why were you sleeping in my class?'

'I guess it was boring, sir.'

The class found this very funny.

'Get out, Katsonis,' Mr Kennett snapped.

As Alex headed for the door, Katrina raised her hand.

'Yes, Katrina?'

'If I find the lesson boring, can I go too?'

The class roared with laughter. Mr Kennett's face went red with anger. 'You can both go to the principal's office.'

'Yes sir. Thank you, sir.'

With the radio hidden behind her back, Katrina followed Alex out.

Inside the flying ship, Paul and Riana listened anxiously to Gryvon's voice coming from the Eyestone: 'Gallia, return to the castle at once.'

'They'll be after us soon,' Paul said anxiously.

'Why don't you try and contact your friends?' Riana suggested.

Alex and Katrina ran into the trees that bordered the playing fields.

'That was great,' Alex chortled. 'I thought Kennett was going to explode.'

Katrina turned the radio on and they were rewarded with the sound of Paul's voice. 'Katrina? Alex? Come on, guys. Talk to me. Please?'

Alex grabbed the radio. 'Paul, it's Alex. I can hear you! Speak to me, big buddy!'

'Alex!' Paul yelled into the Eyestone. 'Mate, I never thought I'd be so happy to hear your voice. You're never going to guess what's happened to me ...'

'You went through an energy doorway,' he

299

heard Katrina say. 'You're in a parallel world and you need our help to get home.'

'Right,' Paul said, wondering how she knew so much.

'We're with you all the way, buddy,' Alex said. 'Just tell us what you need. Over.'

'I've escaped from a castle in a flying ship with my friend Riana. We have to be careful what we say. The walls have ears.'

'We copy, Big Eagle,' Katrina said. 'Use the scrambler. Do you copy?

'That's a big ten four, Holmes and Watson,' Paul replied. 'Remember the school camp cave? I'm on my way there now. Imperative you rendezvous there with a conductive cable.'

'Of the flying fox type?' Alex asked.

'Got it in one, Einstein.'

'Comprendez, amigo. On our way. E.T.A., A.S.A.P.'

Lukan, Marna and Ashka were staring at the Eyestone in the Regents' chamber, totally confused by the coded conversation between Paul and his friends.

'What are they saying?' Lukan asked Ashka.

'They may be planning to invade us.'

'The boy must be stopped.' Lukan thumped the table angrily.

Ashka bowed and hurried out. She raced through the castle and down into the deserted power chamber. Ashka went to the trolley beneath the arch and started filling a bag with fresh powerstones. As she worked, Paul's voice came from her Eyestone.

'Regents, I know you can hear all this and it must seem pretty weird. But I'm not the one you have to be afraid of. Listen to this.'

Ashka was shocked to hear her own voice coming from the Eyestone: 'The Regents are fools. They have let the people lose respect for the Spellbinders. Paul, you have no choice in this...'

Gryvon raced in. 'It's Paul's picture box,' he panted.

Ashka realised that Paul was using his video-camera to replay their conversation and inform the Regents of her plan to take over the Spellbinders.

'... Tell me how to make gunpowder,' her

voice continued from the Eyestone.

'The Regents can hear it,' Gryvon wailed. 'Do something!'

Ashka energised her power suit and hurled a bolt at the top of the massive arch. There was a deafening bang and a blinding flash of light.

The explosion reverberated through the castle and all the lights went out. For the first time in living memory, energy ceased crackling around the tower on the castle roof.

Riana held the video-camera speaker close to the Eyestone in the flying ship. 'You want the gunpowder to use against the Regents,' Paul's recorded voice said. 'You want to rule the Spellbinders ...'

The powerstone in the ship floor stopped rotating and the controls went dead in Paul's hands.

'The power's gone,' Paul cried. The flying ship tilted and began a nose-dive. 'We're going down,' Paul yelled to Riana. 'Brace yourself against the wall of the ship and put your head between your knees.'

'Why?'

'It's what flight attendants tell you to do in an emergency.'

'What's a flight attendant?'

'Riana! Just do it!'

As the ground raced up to meet them, Paul stuck his head between his knees and closed his eyes. Riana did the same.

'Big Eagle, do you copy?' Alex yelled into the radio.

There was no reply.

Katrina took the radio from him. 'Paul, are you alright?' All she heard was static.

'I told you two to go to the office,' Mr Kennett said angrily.

Alex and Katrina scrambled to their feet. 'Sorry, Mr Kennett. We ... got lost,' Alex said lamely.

'I'll take that.' Mr Kennett snatched the radio from Katrina.

'But, sir ...'

'Quiet! I'm especially disappointed in you, Katrina. I want you both to go to the principal's office now. I'll be there when the class is over.'

'Yes sir.'

Mr Kennett watched them go.

'Paul's relying on us to get to the cave,' Alex said. 'We'll go to my place and ask Nick to take us.'

'What about Mr Kennett?' Katrina asked. 'What about our parents?'

'No sweat. When we get Paul back, they'll forget all about this. We'll be heroes.'

Mr Kennett was flabbergasted when he saw Alex and Katrina running towards the school gate. 'You two! Stop!' he shouted.

They didn't.

The flying ship lay on its side in a field, torn apart by the crash. Inside was a tangled mess of cables, beams and hull plates. Riana pushed aside a pile of debris and sat up. 'Paul?'

There was a groan.

Riana crawled outside and saw Paul lying under a broken metal beam. 'Are you alright?'

'I think so. I'm glad I listened to that flight attendant.'

'Come on,' Riana urged. 'They'll be looking for us.'

Paul struggled but his leg was trapped under the beam. Riana tried to lift it but to no avail.

'Spellbinder, can I help?'

Paul and Riana looked round and saw a farmer leading an ox towards them. Paul realised he was still wearing the power suit.

'Yes,' he said, putting on an imperious accent. 'I am the Spellbinder Jack. And this is my servant, Jill. A Marauder spell made our flying ship fall from the sky. I am pinned by this beam.'

Riana was dumbstruck by the outrageousness of Paul's lie.

The farmer wrapped his brawny arms around the beam and tried to lift it. Sweat burst out on his forehead but he couldn't budge it.

Static crackled from the Eyestone in Paul's power suit, followed by Ashka's voice: 'All Summoners, listen. Two enemies of the Spellbinders have escaped ...'

Paul yanked the Eyestone from his power suit, fumbled and dropped it. 'Get that for me, servant,' Paul ordered.

As Riana bent to retrieve the Eyestone, she deliberately stood on it. There was a crackle of electricity and the Eyestone went silent.

'Clumsy girl!' Paul yelled. 'Now I can't call for help.' He winked at Riana.

Correon staggered across the dry, rock-strewn landscape of the Wastelands. The sun seemed to pound on his bare head like a blacksmith's hammer. In the distance were the mountains that marked the edge of the Spellbinders' land. Correon knew his only chance of survival was to reach them. But Ashka's flying ship had abandoned him far away. To keep his mind off his raging thirst, Correon put on the headphones of Paul's Walkman and switched it on. He heard Ashka's angry voice.

'... a boy called Paul has stolen a flying ship. He is travelling with a girl called Riana. They must be found and caught.'

'Well done, Paul,' Correon croaked.

Riana held the ox by its nose-ring while the farmer tied a rope around its neck.

'Jack is the youngest Spellbinder I've ever seen,' the farmer remarked.

'He's very clever,' Riana explained. 'But he's got a terrible temper if you keep him waiting.'

The farmer quickly tied the rope around the beam which was trapping Paul. 'I'll have this off you in a moment,' he said respectfully, wrapping his arms around the beam.

'Now!' he called to Riana. 'Pull!'

Riana tugged on the nose-ring but the ox didn't move. She stared directly into its eyes. 'How would you like to be turned into sausages?'

The ox bellowed and started to walk. The beam lifted and the farmer pulled Paul away from the wreck.

'How's your leg?' Riana asked, helping Paul up.

Paul gingerly put his weight on it. 'I can stand. But I don't think I'll be able to walk far.'

'Where is the nearest Healer?' Riana asked the farmer.

'With the timbercutters.'

'We need directions,' Paul said.

'And your ox,' Riana added.

Alex and Katrina were approaching Alex's house when Nick's car reversed rapidly out of the garage. Mr Katsonis hurried out after him. 'You should have tried harder,' he yelled. 'That was a good job.' Nick ignored his father and roared away.

'Looks like Pop found out that Nick got the sack,' Alex said despondently. 'That blows our plan.'

'Maybe we can convince Paul's dad to take us,' Katrina suggested.

'He won't listen.'

'We have to try.'

Paul sat on the ox's back as it ambled along a narrow forest track. He was wearing the power suit under a cloak and carried the videoamera. Riana trudged along beside him.

'Just think,' Paul said, 'by this time tomorrow I could be eating pizza, drinking a chocolate thickshake and watching Star Trek—that's a TV show.'

'Like the news?'

'No, the news is real. It shows all the bad things that have happened that day, like wars and famines and murders.'

'I don't think I'd like your world.'

'At least we don't have Spellbinders.'

Two large, muscular men with axes stepped out of the trees and blocked the track. They glared at Paul.

'What are you doing with Gurp's ox?' one said.

Paul threw back his cloak, revealing the power suit. 'I am the Spellbinder Jack,' he said imperiously.

The timbercutters fell to their knees and bowed to Paul.

'The Spellbinder has hurt his leg,' Riana explained. 'He needs a Healer.'

'Of course, Spellbinder,' said one of the men. 'We'll carry you.'

'I could get to like this,' Paul whispered to Riana.

The rough-hewn log hut was filled with timbercutters and their families. They all stared in silence at Paul who sat at a wooden table laden with food, his bandaged leg propped on a cushion. Riana sat by herself at the back of the room. She scowled as Paul took a bite from a juicy turkey drumstick.

'This is the best turkey I've ever eaten,' Paul announced. 'I thank you, timbercutters, for all your assistance. It will not be forgotten.'

The timbercutters smiled. One of them got to his feet and bowed. 'Spellbinder,' he began nervously, 'we were wondering ...'

'Yes?' Paul prompted, enjoying his role.

'Well, the Spellbinders, in their wisdom, have ordered us to cut a lot of trees for the new bridge. Now we don't have time to cut the firewood we trade for food.'

'There is no shortage of food here,' Paul said, taking another mouthful of turkey.

'That's our winter supply,' the man replied.

'Not that we mind going short,' a woman

said quickly. 'It's an honour to have a Spellbinder in our house.'

Paul guiltily put down the drumstick. 'Then you need not cut any more wood for the Spellbinders,' he declared. 'I, Jack, have decreed it.'

The timbercutters cheered.

A woman holding a baby knelt before Paul. 'My son has not yet been named. Will you give him yours?'

'Of course, you may name him Paul ... I mean Jack.'

'Will you do it with the proper words?'

Paul didn't know what to say.

Riana let him squirm for a moment, then got up. 'Spellbinder Jack is weary from his journey,' she said. 'The ceremony can take place tomorrow.'

Paul gave Riana a grateful look.

'Of course,' a woodcutter said. 'We have prepared a bed.'

Two men carefully lifted Paul and carried him towards a bedroom. Riana followed but a timbercutter stood in her way. 'Servants sleep outside,' he said.

Riana was trying to get comfortable in a pile of damp, prickly hay outside the hut when she heard whispering. She crept to the base of a tree and peered round it. One of the timber-cutters was talking with a leather-clad castle guard.

'But the boy acts like a Spellbinder,' the timbercutter argued.

'He's not,' the guard said. 'He's an imposter. Spellbinder Ashka is on her way. The boy must be held until she gets here.'

'I'll get the others.'

The timbercutter hurried away while the guard kept watch on the front door. Riana quickly crept to the back of the hut to warn Paul. The windows were covered with shutters. Riana looked desperately around and saw a hatchet by a pile of firewood. She grabbed it and used the metal blade to prise open a shutter.

Riana climbed through the window and found Paul sleeping on a bed. She put a hand over his mouth and he woke up, his eyes wide with fear.

'They know who you are,' Riana hissed in

his ear. 'We've got to get out of here!'

As Paul hurriedly began to dress, Riana lifted an oilskin cape from the back of the door.

Riana and Paul hurried along a trail away from the timbercutters camp. Paul was wearing the oilskin cape to hide the power suit.

'Hurry up,' Riana urged Paul, who was starting to lag behind.

'The power suit's heavy.'

'Then take it off and leave it.'

'I can't. It's Correon's.'

'You just like the way people treat you when you're wearing it,' Riana grumbled. She started walking faster.

Paul limped after her. His injured leg was still sore. 'What's bugging you?'

'I'm hungry. '

'You should have said something. There was plenty of food.'

'You should have noticed.'

'I was just trying to act like a Spellbinder.'

'You forgot all about me! Correon would have at least made sure I was fed.'

Paul realised she was right. He had nothing

to complain about: Correon had been banished to the Wastelands.

The smell of water hit Correon like a physical blow. He staggered into the hollow and fell to his knees at the edge of a muddy pool. Dipping his hands into the cool liquid, he scooped some into his mouth. It tasted of acid and he spat out the putrid muck. He tried to get up but his strength was gone. His legs buckled and he collapsed.

Brian Reynolds' car was parked in the driveway. Christine was helping her father tape a poster to the car door. On it was Paul's photograph and the words 'Have you seen this boy?'

'Mr Reynolds,' Katrina called, 'We've found Paul!'

Brian and Christine looked round as Alex and Katrina hurried up to them. 'Where?' Brian asked eagerly.

'In a parallel world,' Alex replied.

'He's on the run from some people called Spellbinders,' Katrina explained.

Brian glared at them.

'It's true, Mr Reynolds,' Alex insisted. 'We were speaking to him on a radio but our teacher confiscated it.'

'Paul needs our help to get home,' Katrina said urgently. 'We need to go back up to the cave. You've got to drive us. Now.'

Christine excitedly grabbed her father's hand. 'Let's go, Dad.'

'Just a moment, sweetheart.'

Brian took Alex and Katrina aside. 'Listen,' he said fiercely, 'Paul is not in the Twilight Zone. He's lost and I'm doing everything I can to find him. I don't need two teenagers with overactive imaginations making our lives any more difficult. If you really want to help, hand out some of these.' He gave them some posters and went back towards the house. 'Come inside, Christine.'

'What about Paul?' Christine asked.

'I'm sorry, sweetheart. They made a mistake.'

'It's hopeless,' Katrina said as Brian and Christine went into the house. 'We'll never get up to the cave in time.'

'There's always the last resort of modern youth,' Alex said. 'Public transport—we can take a train.'

Paul and Riana trotted along a path between ploughed fields. They heard the throbbing of a flying ship and dived into the undergrowth beside the path.

'They've turned the power system back on,' Paul said grimly as the ship flew overhead. 'We're sitting ducks on this track.'

Riana pointed to a bend ahead. 'There's a bridge just up there. Once we get across it, we'll be safe. It's forest all the way to Clayhill.'

The throbbing of the flying ship faded as it disappeared over the trees.

'Let's go,' Paul said.

They ran along the track to the bend. Ahead was a narrow wooden bridge, guarded by three men. Riana and Paul were about to turn back when Gryvon rode around the bend behind them with more men. Riana raised her hatchet.

'There are too many,' Paul said. 'Follow me.'

He threw back his oilskin cape and charged the guards at the bridge, yelling at the top of his voice. Riana ran after him, yelling and brandishing the hatchet.

The guards were unnerved by the sight of a boy in a power suit and a crazed girl charging them. They ran for their lives.

As Paul and Riana were crossing the bridge, Ashka appeared at the far side. Paul and Riana stopped and looked back. Gryvon was approaching from the other end with the guards. They were trapped in the middle

'Give up, Paul,' Gryvon yelled, 'and we'll let Riana go back to Clayhill.'

'He's lying,' Riana said.

Paul took off his cape and quickly wrapped the video-camera in it.

'What are you doing?'

'Trying to keep the camera from getting wet. We're going for a swim.'

Paul pulled the powerstones from the suit and dropped them off the bridge. There was a crackle of electricity as they hit the water. 'Come on.'

As Paul and Riana climbed onto the railing, Ashka and Gryvon started running towards them. Paul looked nervously at the water rushing below.

'After you,' he said to Riana.

Riana shook her head. 'It was your idea.'

Paul took Riana's hand and they jumped. Ashka and Gryvon reached the middle of the bridge and looked down. All they could see was rushing water.

Riana struggled to keep afloat as the current carried her away from the bridge. She was swept through rapids, crashing from rock to rock, and tumbled down a waterfall. She fell through the air and splashed into a calm pool. She surfaced and looked around.

'Paul!' she called anxiously.

There was a splash as Paul dropped into the pool behind her. Riana dragged him to the shore and they lay on the muddy bank, regaining their breath. Paul was still clutching the video-camera wrapped in the oilskin.

'Come on,' Riana urged. 'we're almost there.' She helped him up and they staggered into the trees.

Correon lay on his back under the hot sun, barely breathing. He would not give up the struggle to live but he didn't have the strength to get up. A shadow fell across his face. He opened his eyes and squinted against the glare of the sun. Two figures were standing over him. They knelt beside him, and Correon realised it was Kurn and Zander.

'What do you mean there's a train strike?' Alex yelled at the station attendant. 'This is an emergency, you idiot.'

Before the angry man could shut the ticket office window, Katrina pushed Alex aside. 'I'm sorry, sir,' she said sweetly. 'Could I please have two tickets for the first train tomorrow.' she slid some money under the window.

'But what if Paul's at the cave already?' Alex protested. 'He's expecting us to be there.'

'What choice do we have?'

Alex shrugged. The attendant gave Katrina the tickets.

'Come round and get me at six,' Katrina said

as they walked out of the station.

'OK. And I'll find a metal cable. What are you going to tell your parents?'

'I'll make up some story. See you then.' She started to head for home.

'Katrina,' Alex called after her, 'you were right about Paul. I'm sorry I didn't believe you sooner.'

'Thanks.' Katrina gave Alex a big smile. Maybe he wasn't such a jerk after all.

It was well after nightfall when Paul and Riana reached Clayhill. They stood among the trees at the edge of the village, tired and hungry. The lights shining from the cottage windows looked warm and welcoming.

'Your parents are going to be surprised to see us,' Paul said.

'We can't let them see us. If they don't know about us, the Spellbinders won't hurt them.'

'But that means you can't go home. Ever. What will you do?'

'I don't know. Come on. Let's just go to the

Summoning Tower and send you back.' Riana sadly turned away from her home.

'We can't,' Paul said. 'I need a length of chain to short out the tower and open the doorway.'

Riana thought for a moment. 'In the village barn, there's a chain that turns the grinding stone. Maybe we can get that.'

Paul and Riana crept into the village and made their way to the barn. They eased inside the door and waited. There was no sound. Riana led Paul to the waterwheel. A heavy chain ran from the wheel to turn the millstone that ground Clayhill's wheat into flour. 'Will this do?' she whispered.

Paul examined the chain, looking for a joining link. There wasn't one. 'Yes. But I'll have to break a link to get it off the wheel. I wish you guys had metal hammers.'

As Paul started looking for a suitable implement, Riana remembered the hatchet in the pocket of her cloak.

'What about this?'

'Brilliant!' Paul took the hatchet and swung it at the chain. There was a tremendous clang as metal struck metal.

'Who's there?' a voice called from the back of the barn.

Paul and Riana dived into the shadows just as Bron came out of a cow stall. He saw the hatchet lying by the chain and picked it up.

'Come out,' he called again and was surprised to see his daughter appear. He dropped the hatchet and hugged her tightly, tears welling in his eyes. 'Riana! I thought I'd never see you again. The Summoner said the Spellbinders are chasing you. I'm glad you're not with Paul.'

'Hello, Bron,' Paul said as he emerged from the shadows.

'Because of you the Spellbinders want to banish my daughter!' Bron grabbed Paul and started pushing him towards the barn door.

Riana stood in his path. 'Da, what are you doing?'

'Taking him to the Summoner. If I hand him in, perhaps they'll show you mercy.'

'Da, no!'

The Final Challenge

'Paul hasn't done anything wrong,' Riana protested.

Bron ignored her and dragged Paul towards the door of the barn.

'He saved my life, remember?' Riana pleaded. 'And Jal's. He drove away the Marauders. He deserves a chance to get home. You have to help him. Please!'

Bron hesitated.

'Da, if Paul goes back to his world, the Spellbinders will leave us alone.'

Bron looked at his daughter and realised she was telling the truth. 'I know I'm going to regret this,' he said, letting Paul go. 'How can I help?'

Paul pointed to the chain around the millstone. 'I need that to take that up to the Summoning Tower to open the doorway to my world.'

Bron shook his head. 'If you break it, how will we grind our grain?'

'The metal is soft,' Paul said. 'Once I've gone, you can melt the links over a hot fire and rejoin them.'

Bron sighed and took the hatchet from Riana. 'Stand back.'

Sparks flew as the blade bit into the chain. Riana turned to Paul. 'I hope this works.'

'If Alex and Katrina have got the cable rigged in my world, I think it will.' Paul sounded more confident than he felt.

Bron continued to hack at the chain. None of them noticed the Summoner peering through the slats in the barn wall.

'Hey, Mum,' Alex called as he came into his floodlit backyard and saw his mother hanging up the washing. 'Has Dad got any old steel cable lying around?'

'How should I know? Ask him when he gets home from work. Help me with this.'

Alex pulled a wet shirt from the basket. As

he pegged it up, he realised that the clothes line was made of steel cable.

'You go and have a cup of tea, Mum,' he said, taking the basket. 'I'll finish this.'

'You're a good boy, Alex.'

As soon as his mother was inside the house, Alex started taking the wet clothes off the line.

'I saw the boy washed away,' Gryvon told the Regents in their chamber. 'He can't have survived.'

'The threat of invasion from his world is gone,' Ashka concluded.

A voice came from the Eyestone on the wall: 'Spellbinders, this is the Summoner of Clayhill. The boy Paul and Riana are in my village.'

The Regents stared at Ashka.

'You must be mistaken, Father,' Gryvon said into the Eyestone.

'I'm not. They're with the girl's father now.'

'Hold them until I arrive,' Ashka ordered. Before the Regents could say anything, she bowed and went out. Gryvon followed.

'Don't worry,' Gryvon said as they hurried along the corridor. 'This time Paul won't escape.'

'I don't care about the boy,' Ashka snapped. 'It's what's in his picture box that's important. If the Regents ever hear the rest of what I said, we'll both be banished. Get some spare power-stones and meet me at the flying ships.' Gryvon ran down the stairs towards the power chamber.

In the courtyard, Apprentices were loading a flying ship with crop-dusting chemicals. Ashka strode out of the castle and climbed into the ship.

'Elrik, I need this flying ship,' Ashka barked at the Spellbinder in the control chair.

'You can't have it. There's an outbreak of the red blight in Orkard.'

'Forget the blight! I need the ship!'

'So do I!'

Ashka and Elrik glared at each other. Then Ashka smiled. 'I'm sorry I was rude. But this is urgent. Perhaps you could take me to the Summoning Tower at Clayhill. It's on your way, isn't it?'

Bron brought the hatchet down again and the chain broke. Riana stifled a yawn.

'You look exhausted,' Bron said. 'Go and get some sleep. And take this back with you.'

He held out a jar containing a clear liquid.

'What is it?'

'Sleeping potion. I was tending a sick cow when you arrived.'

Riana took the jar and went out of the barn.

'Now tell me why the Spellbinders are hunting you and my daughter,' Bron said to Paul.

Paul took the camera from his pack and switched it on. Bron was astounded by the pictures on the screen. When he heard Ashka plotting to overthrow the Regents, his amazement turned to anger. 'Now I see why Ashka is after you,' he said grimly. 'What will you do with this?'

'I want Riana to show it to the Regents.'

'No! It's too dangerous.'

'She must. Otherwise she'll be hunted by Ashka for the rest of her life.'

'Just a short time ago Riana was a happy girl, without a care in the world,' Bron said sadly.

'Then you arrived and everything changed. You have brought great pain to this family.'

'I'm sorry, Bron. I didn't mean for any of this to happen.'

'I believe you. But I wish you had never come to my village.'

Bron began removing the chain from the millstone. Feeling wretched, Paul bent to help him.

Inside the garage, Alex was splicing together the lengths of cable he'd cut from the washing line. Wet clothes hung on nails around the walls. There was a knock on the door.

'Alex,' his mother called. 'It's your girlfriend.'

Alex opened the door a fraction. His mother was outside with the cordless phone.

'I haven't got a girlfriend,' he said, then realised who it must be. 'Thanks, Mum,' he smiled, taking the phone.

He closed the door and spoke into the phone. 'Hi, Katrina.'

'I can't come with you tomorrow,' Katrina said unhappily. 'I've been grounded.'

'Why?'

'Mr Kennett phoned and told Mum we nicked off from school.'

'Did you tell her why?'

'Yeah. And she thinks I'm nuts. I have to see a psychologist tomorrow.'

'But you've got the train tickets!'

Before Katrina could reply, her mother's voice came on the phone. 'Who is this?' she demanded.

Alex looked at his watch. 'At the beep the time will be 7.56 and 30 seconds,' he intoned in a deep voice. 'Beep.'

The phone went dead in his ear.

Riana was asleep in a chair by the fire when Bron and Paul came into the cottage. As Paul put the chain down on the table, the iron links clanked together, waking Riana. She got up and began ladling hot stew into bowls.

'This will be our last meal together,' she said to Paul sadly.

Arla looked up sleepily from her bed. 'Riana,' she cried. 'The Spellbinders are after you. You've got to hide.'

'It's alright, Arla. They don't know I'm here.'

Arla got up and came into the living area. She stopped when she saw Paul. 'Ma hates you. She says you put a spell on Riana.'

'He didn't,' Bron told her. 'Go to bed.'

Arla turned and bumped the table. The end of the chain fell off and unravelled noisily onto the floor.

'I think we should go,' Paul said, gathering it up.

But the damage was done. Maran came out of the sleeping area and saw Paul. Her eyes widened with fear as she noticed the power suit under his cape. 'It's true. You have stolen a power suit.'

'You don't have to worry,' Paul assured her. 'It doesn't work.'

'Don't worry?' Maran cried in anguish. 'The Spellbinders are hunting my daughter!'

'Ma, you don't understand,' Riana said.

'Quiet!' Maran shouted.

'Maran, sit down and listen.' Bron took Maran's arm but she threw his hand off and turned angrily on Paul.

'What have you done to my daughter?'

'Nothing. The Spellbinder Ashka has been lying.'

Maran put her hands over her ears. 'I won't hear any more. I'm going to fetch the Summoner.'

She moved towards the door but Riana got there first. Maran pushed Riana away but before she could open the door, it flew back and the Summoner came in with three men. He pointed at Paul and Riana. 'Bind them.'

Paul threw his cloak aside and the men stopped, eyeing the power suit in fear.

'The first one who moves gets blasted,' Paul threatened. 'Riana, take the chain and go.'

Riana stepped towards the table.

'He can't hurt you, Summoner,' Maran said. 'The power suit doesn't work.'

Paul groaned.

'Take him,' the Summoner ordered.

The men rushed Paul, pushed him to the

ground and began to remove the power suit.

'Let him go,' Riana pleaded. 'He's just trying to get home.'

Riana went to Paul's aid but she was dragged away. The men tied Paul's and Riana's wrists.

'Don't hurt my daughter,' Bron cried.

'Take him too,' the Summoner commanded.

'But Bron has done nothing,' Maran protested.

'I saw him in the barn helping them,' the Summoner said. 'He must be judged by the Spellbinders.'

A distraught Maran gathered Jal and Arla close. Her life was falling apart and she was unable to do anything about it.

The sun had just risen as Alex hurried towards Katrina's house, carrying the cable. He stopped outside the house and looked around. There was no sign of Katrina. He noticed two paper aeroplanes on the street. Then another one landed nearby. Alex opened it. Written on the

paper were the words GO TO SIDE OF HOUSE—
UPSTAIRS WINDOW. KAT.

Alex grinned and sneaked down the side of
the house. Katrina was looking out of an
upstairs window. She put her finger over her
lips and held up two train tickets. She mimed
climbing a ladder and then pointed to the
shed at the back of the house.

Alex gave her the thumbs up and sneaked
towards the shed. As he reached the kitchen
window, he got down on his knees and
crawled through the flower bed beneath it.
Suddenly the window opened and Mrs
Muggleton emptied a teapot on to the
flowerbed. The wet leaves landed on Alex's
head. He forced himself to remain still until
the window closed, then got up and ran
towards the shed.

Paul, Riana and Bron sat on the floor of the
cottage, their hands bound. The Summoner
nervously paced the room. His men guarded
the door. Maran sat comforting Jal and Arla.

333

She jumped as Ashka's voice boomed from the Summoner's Eyestone. 'Summoner, I will be at Clayhill shortly. If you let the boy escape, I will burn your village.'

Maran gasped at the threat.

'Hold the girl and her family as well,' Ashka continued. 'They are all enemies of the Spellbinders and must be punished.'

'No,' Maran wailed in despair. 'I have always been true to the Spellbinders.'

'Summoner, Ashka is lying,' Paul cried. 'This family has done nothing wrong.'

The Summoner shook his head. 'I must obey the Spellbinder.'

Maran glared at Paul. 'This is all your doing.'

'No, Ma,' Riana protested. 'He's telling the truth.'

'That's enough,' Maran cried.

'She's your daughter,' Bron pleaded. 'She loves you. Why do you believe the Spellbinder and not her?'

Maran turned away from Bron and Riana and was silent for a moment. Then she smiled at the Summoner. 'Summoner,' she said calmly. 'Let me make you and your men some tea while you wait.'

Riana couldn't bear to watch as her mother prepared the tea.

'Thank you, Maran,' the Summoner said. 'I will ask the Spellbinder Ashka to show you mercy.' He sipped his tea.

Maran poured cups for his men, never once looking at her husband or daughter.

Alex crawled awkwardly back beneath the kitchen window dragging an aluminium ladder. He carefully positioned it against the wall and Katrina climbed down.

'Isn't this going to get you in a heap of trouble?' Alex whispered.

'Like you said, when we bring Paul back, we'll be heroes.'

They hurried away from the house.

Maran moved warily across the cottage. The Summoner was sitting by the fire, his eyes closed. She nudged him with her toe but he was fast asleep. So were his men. Maran went to Riana and started to untie her.

'What did you do to them?' Riana asked in amazement.

'I put the cow's sleeping potion in their tea. I never thought the Spellbinders could be cruel, but Ashka wanted to punish my family—I couldn't let her do that.'

Maran untied Bron's arms and he hugged her. Riana untied Paul. 'Ashka will be here soon,' she said, 'you must go.'

Paul gave the video-camera to Bron. 'If you show the tape to the Regents, they'll banish Ashka, and your family will be safe.'

Bron nodded. Riana picked up the chain. 'Come on.'

'No, Riana,' Paul said, 'it's too dangerous. Take your family and hide. Once Ashka finds I'm gone, she might come looking for you.'

'Paul's right.' Bron took the chain from Riana and gave it to Paul. He and Maran started putting supplies into bags.

Riana took Paul's hand. 'I'll always

remember you, Paul. You opened my eyes.'

'Same for me,' Paul said. 'I used to think that girls were the weaker sex.'

Riana's smile faded as they heard the throbbing of an approaching flying ship. 'Go,' she urged.

Alex and Katrina ran out of the railway station. The country town was quiet.

'The camp's miles away,' Alex said desperately. 'It'll take us ages to walk there.'

A nun came out of the station behind them, struggling to carry two heavy shopping bags.

'Can we help you with those?' Katrina asked.

'Thank you, dear. That would be very kind.'

Katrina nudged Alex. They each took a bag and followed the nun to the car park.

'What are you doing?' Alex whispered to Katrina.

'If we make up a sob story, maybe she'll give us a lift.'

'Like what?'

'I don't know. You're good at making up stories.'

'Katrina, I can't lie to a nun.'

The nun opened the boot of her old green car and they put the bags inside.

'And what brings you up here?' the nun asked Alex.

Alex opened his mouth but no words came out.

'He's mute,' Katrina said quickly.

'No, I'm not. We're trying to save a friend who's trapped in a parallel world. He can't get back and we're his only hope.'

Katrina stared at Alex in horror.

'We need a lift to the Mount Lara school camp,' Alex continued. 'Will you take us? Please?'

'It all sounds very exciting,' the nun replied. 'Hop in the car. You can explain all about it on the way.'

Alex grinned at Katrina, not believing their luck.

Gryvon pushed open the door to Riana's cottage and was surprised to see the Summoner and his men fast asleep. While Gryvon tried to rouse his father, Ashka searched the cottage.

'They're not here,' she said furiously. 'Search the village. I want the boy and I want the picture box.'

As Ashka stormed out, Gryvon saw the power suit lying on the floor. He smiled and pulled a fresh powerstone from his bag.

Hidden in the loft, Riana and her family watched as Ashka searched the lower level of the barn, smashing pots and hurling implements aside in her fury. Gryvon came in, wearing the power suit.

'Search up there,' Ashka snarled, pointing to the loft.

Gryvon started to climb the ramp, then stopped. 'Ashka, Paul's trying to get back to his own world. He'll go to the Summoning Tower. That's where he tried before.'

'Come on.' Ashka ran out of the barn with Gryvon hot on her heels.

In the loft, Bron and Maran sighed with relief. Riana got to her feet.

'Where are you going?' Maran asked.

'To help Paul.'

She moved towards the ramp but Bron grabbed her wrist. 'No, girl. You've done enough.'

'Please, da,' Riana begged.

Paul hung from the ladder on the Summoning Tower, wrapping the chain around a crossbeam near the top. He climbed back to the ground and picked up the other end of the chain. He dropped it over the metal dish on the stand at the base of the tower. Sparks flew as power surged down the chain and struck the dish.

There was a ripping sound and the air behind the stand seemed to thicken. Paul watched eagerly as the doorway between the two worlds began to open. He cautiously touched the energy curtain, but his hand wouldn't go through. Without the cable on the other side, he could not go home.

'Alex,' he called in frustration. 'Where are you?'

The nun's car stopped outside the school camp and Alex and Katrina climbed out.

'Thanks for the lift, Sister Josephine,' Katrina said.

'Not at all. I enjoyed hearing your story. I love science fiction.'

Alex and Katrina looked at each other in confusion.

'But if you needed a lift,' the nun continued, 'you should just have asked me. You shouldn't tell fibs, especially to nuns.'

'No, sister.' Alex said repentantly. Even when he told the truth, no-one believed him.

'Enjoy the camp. And may the force be with you.' Chuckling to herself, the nun drove off.

Alex and Katrina hurried towards the cave.

Paul anxiously paced the ground near the

tower, watching the partially opened doorway.

'Have your friends deserted you?'

Paul whirled around and saw Ashka standing at the head of the trail to Clayhill. He backed away but Gryvon grabbed him from behind. He searched Paul's clothes. 'He hasn't got the picture box.'

'Where is it?' Ashka demanded.

Paul pointed towards the stand at the base of the tower.

'Get it,' Ashka commanded.

Gryvon followed Paul to the stand. Paul bent, pretending to pick something up. As he straightened, he shoved Gryvon against the sparking chain. Energy crackled around Gryvon's power suit and he was thrown to the ground. Paul ran for the rocks.

'I'll get him,' Gryvon yelled, and raced after Paul.

Ashka was about to follow when she heard Katrina's voice coming from her Eyestone.

'Paul, it's Katrina. We're at the cave. Are you there?'

'I can hear you, Katrina,' Ashka said into her Eyestone. 'I am Riana. A friend of Paul's.'

'Is Paul with you?' Katrina asked.

'He's on his way now,' Ashka lied.

'Great. Is it safe to open the doorway?'

'Yes. But you'd better hurry. The Spell-binders are coming. Paul's in danger.'

Katrina and Alex stood by the cave, watching the energy flickering in the air.

'We have to rig the cable,' Katrina said into the radio. 'Tell Paul we won't be long.' She turned to Alex who was fixing one end of the cable in the cave mouth. 'How long before we're ready?'

'We have to make sure everything is just like it was the first time,' Alex replied. 'The other end of the cable has to go up there.' He pointed to the tree under the high-tension power lines. They started unrolling the cable.

Paul raced along a narrow rock passage but it came to a dead-end. As he looked frantically

343

for a way out, Gryvon appeared. He smiled when he saw that Paul was trapped. 'You stole my power suit,' he said menacingly. 'And you made me look like a fool in front of Ashka. I'm sure she won't mind if I bring you back a little the worse for wear.'

Paul desperately tried to climb the steep rock wall but he slipped back to the ground. Gryvon energised his power suit—but nothing happened.

'Your powerstone shorted out,' Paul said. 'We're even.'

Gryvon smiled and shook his head. 'No, Paul. I brought some more.'

Gryvon took a fresh powerstone from his bag. He was about to fit it to the suit when there was a whirring sound and a set of bolas wrapped around his arm.

Riana jumped down from the rocks and pulled the cord attached to the bolas, preventing Gryvon from fitting the powerstone.

'I order you to let me go,' Gryvon yelled, pulling on the cord with all his strength.

'Yes, Apprentice,' Riana said, and let go of the cord.

Gryvon lost his balance and stumbled backwards. He hit his head on a rock and collapsed to the ground, unconscious.

'Am I glad to see you,' Paul said to Riana. 'Ashka's at the tower.'

'What are we going to do?' she asked.

Paul looked at Gryvon's power suit.

Katrina stood near the cave, looking up at the tree where Alex was wrapping the end of the cable around a branch. Energy began crackling around the power lines above him.

'Alex, watch out!' Katrina yelled.

Alex saw the danger and started to scramble down the trunk. Katrina dived for cover.

Energy leaped from the power lines and flashed along the cable towards the cave.

Paul was wearing the power suit as he and Riana cautiously approached the Summoning Tower. There was no sign of Ashka. Suddenly there was a brilliant flash of light and the energy doorway opened fully. Through the rippling curtain of energy, Paul's world was visible.

'You'd better go,' Paul said to Riana. 'Ashka's here somewhere.'

They stared at each other, realising this meant goodbye. Riana kissed Paul then ran off before he could react. Paul sadly watched his friend disappear into the rocks then started towards the energy doorway. Ashka appeared from behind the tower and blocked his path.

'I won't let you stop me, Ashka.' Paul struck his wrists together and energised the power suit.

'Do you think you can defeat a Spellbinder?' Ashka laughed as she energised her own suit.

Paul hurled a bolt at Ashka but she easily avoided it. Paul desperately threw another. Ashka whirled and fired a bolt, scoring a direct hit on Paul's powerstone. The suit shorted out with a flash and Paul was thrown to the ground.

'You're not going home, Paul,' Ashka said. 'Ever.'

She fired a bolt at the top of the Summoning Tower. There was a shower of sparks, and pieces of metal crashed to the ground. The energy doorway flickered.

'The video-camera's on its way to the Regents,' Paul croaked as he got up. 'When they see the tape, you're finished in this world.'

Ashka looked at the energy doorway and smiled. 'If I'm finished in this world then I'll go to yours.' She strode towards the doorway.

Riana leaped out of the rocks, whirling her bolas. She let them go and they flew through the air, wrapping around Ashka's legs. Ashka sprawled on the ground.

There was another shower of sparks from the tower and the doorway flickered again.

'Go, Paul,' Riana yelled, 'before it's too late.'

Paul gave Riana a last grateful look, then ran towards the doorway and dived through.

Ashka pulled the bolas off her legs and got up. Riana stood defiantly before the open doorway.

'Get out of my way!' Ashka roared.

Riana didn't move. Ashka energised her

power suit. Riana closed her eyes, waiting for the bolt to hit her.

Behind her, Paul's arms reached through the doorway. He grabbed Riana and pulled her through into his world just as Ashka hurled the bolt.

Paul pulled Riana to the ground just as Ashka's power-bolt flew through the doorway. It exploded harmlessly against the rocks above their heads.

Through the flickering doorway, Paul could see Ashka striding towards them. 'Ashka's coming,' he yelled to Alex and Katrina. 'We've got to close the doorway. Pull the cable down!'

Alex ran to the steel cable but power was still crackling around it. He couldn't even get close.

Ashka was only a few steps from the doorway
when a huge shower of sparks erupted from

the top of the Summoning Tower. The tower buckled where her bolt had hit. Ashka hurriedly covered her head with her arms as chunks of hot metal fell from above. One struck the chain and knocked it to the ground. Ashka screamed with frustration as the doorway faded and closed.

Alex and Katrina ran to Paul and helped him to his feet.

'Are you OK?' Alex asked.

'Thanks to you two,' Paul said. He hugged his two friends fiercely. 'I'm home!' He couldn't wait to tell his father all about his adventures.

Still dazed, Riana went over to where the doorway had been.

'Who's the spunk?' Alex asked.

'Grow up,' Paul said. He went over to Riana. 'These are my friends, Alex and Katrina. Guys, this is Riana. I owe her my life.'

'Are all the girls in your world as pretty as you?' Alex asked.

Katrina elbowed him hard in the ribs and smiled at Riana. 'I'm really glad to meet you, Riana. I can't wait to hear all about your world.'

Riana looked desperately at Paul. 'I must go back.'

'You can't,' Paul said gently. 'The doorway's closed. Ashka destroyed the Summoning Tower.'

Riana looked at Paul in horror. 'I'm trapped here?'

'Don't worry. My father's a scientist: he'll get the doorway open again. Now you can see my world.'

The worried look remained on Riana's face. Katrina took her hand. 'Don't worry, Riana. You'll be safe with us.'

'Hey, Paul,' Alex said excitedly, 'we can make megabucks out of this. We can sell the story to the newspapers.' He spelt out an imaginary headline: '"Lost Girl from the Land of the Spellbinders." You'll be on the front page, Riana. I bet you'll look great in a swimsuit.'

'Alex!' said Paul and Katrina together.

'Yeah?'

'Shut up.'